W9-CRC-298

RAWI HAGE

STRAY DOGS

Stories

ALFRED A. KNOPF CANADA

PUBLISHED BY ALFRED A. KNOPF CANADA

Copyright © 2022 Rawi Hage

www.penguinrandomhouse.ca

The author gratefully acknowledges the Canada Council for the Arts
for a grant providing assistance during the writing of this book.

Canada Council   Conseil des arts
for the Arts   du Canada

Library and Archives Canada Cataloguing in Publication

Title: Stray dogs : stories / Rawi Hage.
Names: Hage, Rawi, author.
Identifiers: Canadiana (print) 20210258004 | Canadiana (ebook) 20210258012 |
ISBN 9780735273627 (hardcover) | ISBN 9780735273641 (EPUB)
Subjects: LCGFT: Short stories.
Classification: LCC PS8615.A355 S77 2022 | DDC C813/.6 — dc23

Book design by Lisa Jager

Printed in Canada

10 9 8 7 6 5 4 3 2 1

Penguin
Random House
KNOPF CANADA

For Aya.

CONTENTS

THE ICONOCLAST

IN 2011, I WAS OFFERED a writing residency in Berlin. I was given an apartment in Kreuzberg. I worked on a novel in the mornings and smoked outside on the balcony in the afternoons. Whenever I leaned on the edge of the balcony, I would see below me a street, a lamp and a garden. One day when I was out there, a woman standing in the garden waved at me. A moment later, her husband joined in. I waved back and nodded.

During the day, I spent a great deal of time alone, writing and reading. In the evening, it became my custom to join the couple in their garden for a beer or two.

Lukas was an erstwhile photographer. Hannah held a clerical job.

We talked about our lives, politics, books. We exchanged anecdotes and political opinions. Photography was Lukas's profession, but he also had a long history of "involvement with syndicates," and in his youth had been a member of a German anarchist group.

One night, Hannah confided that Lukas had lost hope in the world. He had lost his belief in humanity. He talks about his causes, Hannah told me, but their defeat has been too much to bear. The radical in him has diminished, and he's retreating into himself.

A garden is every warrior's final objective, I said.

I wish he would go back to photography, Hannah said. He was happier back then.

Well, I quipped, every hero is a being without talent. I was quoting the Romanian-French philosopher Cioran, but as soon as I realized my insult, I excused myself and rushed back up to my apartment.

Another night, at a party at Hannah and Lukas's home, a man who looked like Marx — long beard, round face, broad shoulders and belly — approached and asked me what I was writing about. He pulled a handkerchief from his back pocket and patted it on his forehead, then on his cheeks, and finally inflated it loudly with his nostrils.

I said, joking, I am writing about the German soul.

He chuckled, tucked his piece of cloth in his front pocket this time and asked me to explain.

I said, Germans have a distant and cautious approach to strangers, which I prefer to the overly familiar approach to others in French colonial history.

So, presuming the strangeness of others is right in your opinion? he asked.

It allows for curiosity and the possibility of a future dialogue, I replied.

So long as we are curious, he replied, we tend to tolerate.

Indeed, I said. Familiarity breeds contempt, to quote the French novelist Stendhal.

You studied French literature?

I nodded and volunteered that my work dealt with how photographic images appear in literature. The man nodded too and took a sip from his beer. You know, he said. He paused before continuing: This is a tight group. So I was not curious about you, I must admit. I was not interested. If anything, I have some hostility towards your type. I am opposed to the money that our government squanders on foreign artists like you, on getting them to come and live here and spend time on their inconsequential bourgeois projects. This money should go to social programmes. You certainly fit the type they go for. Let me guess: you are French-educated, wealthy — and yet here is our government, sprinkling cash on developing-world, privileged sorts like you. I feel that the money spent on you could easily be put to better use. Because of you and the likes of you, our neighbourhoods now are gentrified, and our Berlin is changing. You are either naive or you're complicit with neoliberal capitalism masquerading as a cultural contribution to the world.

I think you're partially right about who I am, I conceded. But what does our host Lukas think?

The same, he said. We all think the same here about your kind.

I felt like leaving at that moment, but Hannah, who was watching from across the room, came over and led me by the hand into the kitchen. Let's have a photo of the three of us, she said, and she pulled Lukas over.

You looked upset, and I wanted to save you, she said in a low voice. Santa over there can be offensive. Don't listen to him.

Soon after, I left quietly.

The next day, after my afternoon nap and feeling satisfied with the progress of my writing, I went down to the garden for my customary beer with Hannah and Lukas. I sat down and handed Lukas a bottle. We didn't talk about the night before. Over time, I had learned that the strength of a close-knit social group lies in its ability to compartmentalize.

Lukas asked me what I was up to.

I leave tomorrow for Beirut for a conference on photography, I said. You should come and visit my city sometime.

He nodded and replied, I will.

The conference was to be held at the American University of Beirut. I didn't expect many people to attend my lecture, as my subject was not directly related to anything overtly political — the Arab world, the Palestinian cause or any such stressful subjects. Instead, my presentation would be on the final passage in James Joyce's short story "The Dead," and I knew that exploring the topic of the spatial in the work of James Joyce would be seen as an indulgence, a luxury.

In the last scene of the story, the protagonist Gabriel gazes at a window and describes his memories in a gradual visual movement, evoking a series of photographs that simultaneously detail the spatial and the psychological. We see the window, a lamp, the River Shannon and, at the centre of the montage, the burial site of the young Michael Furey, Gabriel's wife's once-upon-a-time lover.

In reviewing this passage, I would emphasize the personal, local and national context of the objects and places we observe, expanding on the mention of the river in this text and in Joyce's work generally, and simultaneously exploring the idea of the photograph as a subject suspended between life and death. I would allude to Barthes's aphorism in *Camera Lucida* that every photograph is an image of what has passed, and I would even dare to say that photography functions as a prophecy of death — overtly linking these observations to the title of Joyce's story, "The Dead."

The more I thought about the presentation of my paper, the more I felt that I was ultimately describing a particular suspended existence — my own. And now I felt the temptation to introduce another metaphor: my own identity as a person perpetually suspended between cultures, religions and geographies. But a part of me also hated that narcissism and opportunism, so prevalent in academia.

After reflecting on this for a while, I concluded that while my work was indeed about ephemerality, it was not about the ephemerality of the self. Rather, it examined the ephemerality of the *image* of the self. Every hybrid was a partial death, an incomplete acquisition of the original.

The day after the party at Lukas and Hannah's — the day before I left for the conference — I strongly felt my state of suspension. All I could think about were the characters in "The Dead," the woman who had lost her first lover for the incomplete acquisition of another, and the inevitability that she would lose them both.

The next day, as I was leaving for the airport, Lukas came out into the garden and said, I booked a ticket to your city. Hannah thought that I should go, since you offered.

Ah! I said. When will you visit?

Wednesday of this week, he said. I want to do some photography in your country.

I'll find you a place to stay, I offered.

Perhaps I can stay at your house?

I am staying with my brother and his family, I explained. But I'll find you another place. A lively neighbourhood, I promised.

Lukas smiled.

My worry was not so much about settling on a suitable place for Lukas to stay but finding the time to exercise the hospitality expected of a local host. Between my family obligations and the presentation of my paper at the American University, I feared he'd be left without a guide. But through my contacts in Beirut, I quickly arranged for Lukas to lodge in a room in a shared house with an acquaintance of mine near Rue Hamra. The two hit it off, and soon they were hanging out at cafés and bars. After a short while, they could be found in the same bar every day. Then Lukas's roommate left on a trip, and he was left alone in the house.

My neighbourhood was on the east side of the city, some distance from where Lukas was staying, but I made time to join him in the afternoon for a drink and to check up on him regularly. He did well on his own, having quickly made friends at the bar. Al-Almaneh, the German, everyone called him. Soon enough, he did not seem to need my help. He was content with the local hospitality.

One afternoon, Lukas admitted to me that Beirut was not what he'd expected in terms of the photographs he'd hoped to take. It was too modern, he said.

I asked if he'd expected to see camels.

He laughed. Then, two days later, he called me on the phone and said someone at the bar had told him he should take photographs in the populous neighbourhood of Dahieh.

I advised against it. I told him that an Islamist militia ran the enclave, that it was the headquarters for this group and was considered a military zone. The moment he pointed a camera, he would be held, interrogated, and his equipment confiscated.

But Lukas was drunk, and he ranted about his love for the oppressed and for those who keep the struggle alive. He declared he was fed up with sitting in the Western bubble of the neighbourhood where he was staying.

I urged him again not to go, but he was stubborn and incoherent and hung up on me.

In the middle of that night, I woke up in a panic.

The idiot, I thought. He will get us in trouble.

I remembered that Lukas had given my name and my brother's address at the airport as references. Once he was stopped and interrogated, as would inevitably happen, the militia would trace him to our home, to my brother's house.

I put on my clothes and called a cab to Hamra. I climbed the stairs to Lukas's apartment and banged at the door. When he opened it, I entered without waiting to be invited.

A Lebanese woman emerged from the kitchen, leaned against the edge of the door and watched me trying to convince Lukas not to go. I gestured and screamed at him, and the woman smiled. She took one step towards me and said, He'll be with me, nothing will happen to him there.

I said, Then he's your responsibility from now on. You deal with it and make sure to tell the militia that my family and I have nothing to do with him.

Yeah, she said. You go back to your beautiful neighbourhood.

And what neighbourhood would that be? I said.

You know, your neighbourhood, she said with sarcasm.

Everywhere is my neighbourhood, I shot back.

Then, what are you people always so afraid of?

Who are "you people"? I asked.

Bourgeois people, Lukas answered, and he and the woman laughed.

Not long after this, my work there done, I left Beirut and went back to Berlin.

A week later, Lukas returned home as well.

I tried to avoid him, but it was awkward because I had to pass in front of his garden every day. And I liked Hannah, who was always welcoming to me. So after a little while, we picked up our customary beer, although less frequently than before. We avoided talk of Beirut.

Then, two days before the end of my residency and my return to Lebanon, we had a curious conversation.

I asked Lukas about the photos he'd taken in Lebanon.

Lukas said that he was quitting photography. The image is the root of all evil, he declared. He launched into a tirade about advertisements and propaganda and oppression, saying that every image we were shown was a form of deceit. And the source of all visual propaganda lay in the Church, he said.

Iconoclasm, I said.

He told me then that he was going back to Beirut. The people he'd met there, he declared, were real, hospitable, genuine.

I wished him luck. I'm sure you'll be in good hands this time, I said.

A year later, my book was published, and I was invited back to Germany for a book tour.

From my Berlin hotel, I took the U-Bahn to Kreuzberg to visit Lukas and Hannah.

I found Hannah at home. Her dog growled at me, then came closer and wagged his tail.

The garden, I noticed, seemed neglected. But Hannah greeted me with her beautiful smile.

Where is the man of the house? I asked.

He left, she said. He no longer lives here.

You two are no longer together?

No. Lukas met a woman from your country and brought her here. They both stayed with me for a while; then it all became too complicated. She has family in Germany, and they were visiting us daily. Her family would come here and stay forever and cook. Her sister and her husband started to sleep here sometimes. The house turned into a commune. Then, one day, I asked everyone to leave.

They went back to Beirut? I asked.

No, they live in Sonnenallee, Arabische Strasse, with the rest of their Arabic friends. Lukas tore all his photographs and burned his archive and his collection of photography books. He changed.

We all change, I said.

No, he changed his religion, she said.

Converted? I asked.

Yes.

Because of her?

No, she had nothing to do with it. If anything, she was surprised by his new zealot self. I don't think she cares about religion. You know what? I even liked her. We did get along; she's young and beautiful, smart, educated and caring.

When I asked Lukas about his conversion, she continued, he launched into a rant about class, imperialism and the role of the image in world culture. He rifled through a shoebox where I kept my family photos and tore them all up. I thought it was his way of breaking with the past. I guess, when people change their lives, old images carry ghosts and haunt them. It's a strange thought. He tore up every single photograph . . . Except the one of the three of us, you and me and Lukas, the one we took that night at the party.

I handed that photo to him and said, You might as well finish the job. But he yelled, NO! I asked him why, but he wouldn't answer. When I pressed him for an answer, he said something strange. He said that you are not one thing. I asked him what he meant. Did he mean that you, the Academic — as we secretly called you — was not one thing? He didn't answer directly, only said he was against what was monolithic, visible. And Islam, I asked, is that not all about unification? At that, he stood up and left. It leads me to think that he may still be searching for that "one thing" — and that neither he nor I know what that is.

Do you think he'll come back? I asked.

No, I can't provide him with what he has now — community, family and a nice girl.

What now? I said, after a pause. What's next for you, Hannah?

Oh, I am moving back to Hamburg. My father is dying. I must take care of him. I have to see my father's image once more. He won't deprive me of that. And I guess I'll get a job and eventually inherit the family home.

And the garden here? I asked.

Everything in nature lives and dies. Just like all religions and beliefs, she said.

I nodded and took my leave. I walked out of the gate and onto the street.

Hannah called after me just before I disappeared around the corner, and I looked back. She asked me to wait a moment, rushed inside and returned with something in her hand. She handed me the photograph she'd taken long ago, of me with her and Lukas in their kitchen at the party. Then she went back down the road and stood at her gate, sad and defeated. You should come and visit me in Hamburg sometime, she said.

But I never did.

BIRD NATION

IT IS AN UNCOMFORTABLE but indisputable fact that the consumption of wheat is behind the current obesity epidemic in Lebanon. Indeed, many studies suggest that genetically modified wheat, in particular, is the decisive factor leading to weight gain, among other mental and physical complications, in the Lebanese population. Let us now thoroughly scrutinize our specimen, the Lebanese citizen, to confirm that wheat and its derivatives is the major contributor to the many troubles of this small nation.

First, we observe that obesity is visible in the nation's rulers, politicians and, most obviously, its clerical class.

Second, we note that the use of utensils at the Lebanese table is not essential. The fork and the spoon were introduced during French rule of the region. But there was no need for these particular items because the Lebanese had long ago found a way to use their thin bread as both a grabbing device and a scooping tool. This traditional practice, one must admit, is an ingenious way of preserving autonomous and hygienic practice in a cuisine that encourages sharing and the communal consumption of food. To explain: Each person rips off a small piece of bread and uses it to handle the food and consume it. He or she will go on to take a new, freshly ripped piece of bread to scoop or grab again. In this manner, every bit of food is consumed, and every stage of consumption uses a new and clean utensil.

There are exceptions to this practice, of course — such as when eating birds. One eats a bird with bare hands and without the use of bread. For such unique occasions a word was invented, *nesh*, which means *eating without bread*.

Lebanon's renowned cuisine could well be considered one of the most diverse and healthy in the world. Well, without the wheat factor, of course. Wheat, or more precisely bread, is the country's misdemeanour, perhaps even its unappreciated tragedy, alongside its unbearable rulers, noise, corruption, the constant threat of war and its mad traffic.

It did not have to be this way. The Lebanese have a great affinity for the taste of birds. Birds are killed indiscriminately, hunted and plucked, opened and emptied of their entrails, and then grilled and served with slices of lemon and lashes of salt. Small birds are often devoured bones and all. One takes a special pride in the cracking of a bone in one's mouth.

Before the devastating effects of the pesticide DDT, widely deployed and still in use in what little agricultural space is left in this small country, birds were found in abundance in Lebanon and Syria. But hunters, much like birds, disregard borders in the pursuit of killing, and between the devastating effect of chemicals and the unchecked hunt, the nation's bird population was almost wiped out in the late twentieth century.

Around that time, a cry of alarm went up from environmental organizations and, ironically, from eager hunters — who in the absence of birds had begun turning their guns to imaginary flying goats — and the Lebanese government banned hunting in 1995. This law was effective for a time, and there was a small recovery. But the politicians eventually turned a blind eye to the plight of the birds, the warlords found the law amusing, and the clergy would not challenge widely held beliefs that the earth belongs to humans, nature is in servitude to humanity, and God created birds to be eaten and disposed of by people, et cetera.

Finally, in the absence of birds, the Lebanese went back to consuming the remaining varieties of food, their fingers tearing up and waving around many little pieces of bread. The result was the nation's expansion — each individual's expansion, that is. Soon a nation of rotund midgets could be seen squeezing themselves into their little French-made cars, which they had dearly cherished through the decades. But their wheat bellies and ample asses no longer fit their vehicles. One day, a politician's car had to be dismantled in order to pull him out. Another day, a merchant's wife found herself stuck in her car for hours. As a result, the merchant decided to introduce bigger vehicles to his bread- and car-loving nation: vehicles with four-wheel drive, wider and more seats, higher wheels and larger trunks; cars massive enough to hold a fresh kill, no matter how large. A special feature on one such automobile allowed the trunk to transform into a small seat for the foreign maid who, mysteriously, never gained weight but retained her diminutive size, allowing her to accompany families on their road trips. (We should mention here that, upon further study, it was found that these maids stayed thin and fit because they remained attached to their familiar diets of rice, vegetables and spices.)

Soon enough, the country was filled with large cars. And shortly after that, the popularity of these spacious vehicles triggered an existential crisis among politicians and warlords because customarily this most important strata of society owned the largest cars. Now, the largeness of a vehicle no longer effectively distinguished rulers from the ruled. The car salespeople quickly came up with an ingenious solution: tinted-glass windows! Black glass allowed a vehicle's occupants to see out while remaining shadowy and unrecognizable inside. Within a matter of months, those in the ruling class had acquired tinted windows, and any convoy of five large cars, now with darkened windows, again inspired reverence and signalled importance, even danger. This flock of cars was to be avoided at any cost. If one happened to get in the way, one risked being shot. It was always best to move out of the way and let the power machines pass.

Still, in time, the possession of tinted windows expanded beyond the class of politicians and warlords. Cars belonging to the family members of politicians were, by default, outfitted with tinted windows. The mistresses of warlords found it very convenient to pass incognito through residential neighbourhoods. Eventually, the warlords' favourite singers, as well as ministers' acquaintances and business partners, were granted permission to acquire their own dark shades. People everywhere in the city of Beirut drove around veiled in glass and metal.

Once again, citizens could no longer properly assess wealth, honour and danger. They lost their sense of self-worth, and the invisibility of their status had a devastating, deflating effect on bespoke suit makers, hair gel suppliers, and the purveyors of haute couture, lipstick and high-heeled shoes.

All was gloom in Lebanon until, one day, the clergy made an auspicious announcement: the Pope would visit the country. That April, the arrival of the popemobile liberated the Lebanese from their darkness and isolation.

The popemobile was a revelation. Soon, herds of popemobiles accumulated in Beirut, even on streets known for their taste, fashion and culture, and most of all on those streets famous for the availability of good food.

Wide cubes of transparent glass mounted onto the back of small trucks dotted traffic jams, crawled along the Corniche, through Achrafieh, into the mountains and beyond. Men drove with prideful smiles on their faces and women paraded their latest XXL dresses, lifting their thick ankles to model European heels. In the presence of popemobiles, one heard the Lebs sigh in awe: *There must be a god! After the visit of His Holiness, see how everything flourishes again and the stores are full of enthusiastic shoppers!*

That spring, the hair dryers of stylists never ceased in their generation of wind and money, and the streets glittered with painted nails and colour-soaked toes. *Long live the Pope and his transparent, protective, mobile shrine!* Christians, Muslims and Druze alike could be heard to say these words.

But summer came, and with it the suffocating heat piercing every glass cube, sizzling every trunk and dashboard. Men blasted the air conditioning, to no avail. Inside the pope-mobile *automobile*, sweat condensed like mist on holy water. The merciless sun transformed every car into a spectacular beam of light. Men were forced to exit their cars, carrying their women on their backs. Small streams of water from plastic bottles were poured onto feeble faces. *Lebanon is burning again*, a man was heard to say. *If it is not the war, it is the sun.*

Viewed from the tops of buildings and the cockpits of airplanes, Beirut glittered with the reflections of thousands of glass cubicles. *Oh, here it is, ladies and gentlemen*, one pilot announced to his passengers, *the Paris of the Middle East, the Jewel of the East.*

But *hélas*, brightness viewed from afar is fire when seen up close. A whole nation walked towards the beach, in search of relief. Women divorced their most valuable shoes and dipped their painted, corpulent toes into the Mediterranean waters. Men rolled their large bellies and saggy breasts into the dirty sands as if they were bears, dogs, stranded whales.

People did nothing but eat and listen to their radios. They heard on the news that a beam of light could now be seen continuously shining over Beirut. This light was so bright that an Israeli jet plane, hovering over the city to take photographs, was forced to land. *The pilot*, announced the news broadcast, *was blinded by the power of the light.*

Let's drink to that, the people said, *and let's eat as well! Let's forget about our cars! Let's sell them to the hunters in the villages for a reduced price! If these cars can bring down a plane, imagine what they can do to a bird!*

After a while, the city was emptied of popemobiles, along with the signs and photographs that had welcomed His Holiness.

The same merchant who had come up with the idea of bringing large cars to Lebanon was watching the news on CNN when he saw a large, wide military car. This struck him as the antidote to his past failures.

The HUMMER! he shouted. Yes, that American military vehicle is spacious enough for a family, wide enough for every occupant to be seen, and its open top allows for natural ventilation — meaning that no man or woman will ever be hot again.

The first Hummer that reached Beirut came straight from the desert of Iraq. After a thorough cleaning and a good coat of yellow paint, the merchant drove through town, blasting music by a kitsch singer who had false teeth and, well, false everything. Two young Russian girls were hired to stand on the back seat wearing bikinis. They drank champagne and waved to the crowd.

Within a month, every household owned one or two Hummers. Business people, politicians, warlords, homemakers and mistresses drove these spacious cars. Lines of Hummers expanded into the streets of Beirut like bloated cadavers, getting stuck on sidewalks, or between parked cars, or in the narrow alleys. In frustration, politicians' bodyguards shot into the air, attempting to make space for their employers. But *hélas*, nothing moved. The traffic fell into chronic stillness, a crippling traffic jam that lasted for weeks. Pedestrians were seen crawling beneath Hummers, seeking passage. Small-car owners fearfully ducked bullets from the Hummer owners' guns.

But then, something unexpected occurred.

Ordinary people grew feathers on their back. These feathers thickened into wings, and with every flutter of their new appendages, these people rose until they were floating above the traffic into the air. Flocks of people flapped their wings and learned to fly.

Only the rulers and their entourages — heavy with bread and large cars — did not grow feathers. Only they remained bound to the earth, beneath a nation of colourful citizens flying over the city. They shouted and waved their hands at the flying people above them, but no one noticed anymore. The sky filled with clothes, shoes, falling hats, and wings.

And just then, as the people started to move along, above and away, a politician and his bodyguard lifted their rifles and pointed them at the sky.

STRAY DOGS

WHEN SAMIR MAAROUF was invited to Tokyo to participate in a conference on Japanese photography, he accepted immediately. But then, sitting in his rented house in St. Paul, Minnesota, he wondered: To whom should he break the good news? His parents, in Jordan, would not understand its magnitude. His father, a businessman who commuted to Saudi Arabia for work, was a chain-smoking workaholic who would be pleased at Samir's prospects for travel but wouldn't understand the importance of the invitation to his son's academic career. Like many well-to-do Arabs, Samir had been sent to a university in the United States of America so that he could get a degree in business administration then come back to the Arab world to take care of his father's business. Such a degree was also essential for his mother. She would be able to brag about her child's American education, fill a wall with his graduation picture in a golden frame, gain status in the community, meet him at the airport alongside the entire family and eventually find a suitable bride for her genius of a son.

Samir had therefore shocked the family when he decided to change his major from business to philosophy and write a thesis on photography that would take him three to five years to finish. How would philosophy, or photography for that matter, help in the business world? Samir's father asked with alarm. He thought of photographers as either Armenians or barely one rank above the waiters at a busy wedding. To philosophize about a medium of cheap technological gadgets, to spend three years of one's life writing about a machine that produces an image with the touch of a finger — why would Samir do this? He summoned his son to Jordan. Samir refused to go. His father fought with him over the phone, threatening to cut Samir off, slamming the receiver down in a heated fury; still Samir refused to engage. Furthermore, through his sister, Samir sent his father a message: not only was he willing to be cut off, he'd be content never to go back to Jordan at all.

Samir's father, to make up for the anger that had come out of his mouth smelling of Marlboros and his nightly clandestine glass of Johnnie Walker, anger that had come out mixed with shouts, ice cubes and threats, told his daughter to call her brother and ask him if he needed a good digital camera. He could send one to Samir because in Saudi Arabia these objects were cheap and available in every mall. Samir replied, via his sister, that he hardly ever took photographs, and when he did, he used an old, bulky German camera that produced six-by-six negatives. I mostly *write* about photographs, he told her.

What is there to write about? she asked. Everyone can take a photo.

Julie Golden Wikson, curator and organizer of the Tokyo conference, had specifically asked Samir to present the paper he had published in an art magazine called *Bidan*. The paper was about the Japanese photographer Daido Moriyama and his Czech counterpart, Josef Koudelka.

The "two dogs" paper, Julie clarified. We are interested in the comparison you make between the images that both photographers took, separately, of dogs.

Samir had written that Daido's image of a dog and Koudelka's famous image of another dog, taken in different locations, had the same mythical feel to them. Both images were menacing, Samir had explained. Both were taken at the same high angle, proving they were captured by an erect *Homo sapiens*, a higher being. And both, to Samir's eye, had religious and iconographic references. The devil is present, wrote Samir. In Koudelka's photograph, the pointy dog ears make the animal look like a mythical bat. In Daido's image, the visible teeth and the strong contrast in the black-and-white printing — a characteristic of Daido's style, and of many Japanese photographers of that school and era — make the dog look almost like an eerie, laughing human glancing backwards.

The paper also (predictably, worried Samir) made a comparison between West and East, addressing the religious connotations of both images. The predominance of shadow — or, as Samir wrote, "the praise of shadow" — in Daido's work gave the photo an enigmatic spiritual feel. Daido's intent, thought Samir, was to make the world mysterious and unintelligible and, in the process, to limit understanding of it to the few observers (Samir referred to them as "believers") who would blindly and obediently march the path of obscurity and enlightenment. In Koudelka's case, Samir projected onto the dog's image a mythical shape with strong religious symbolism, a shape that could transcend the abolition of religion in the Communist era, a shape Koudelka had famously experienced and recorded during the Czech uprising of 1968. "To make the devil visible is also to acknowledge the existence of God," Samir wrote in his article.

But what was truly surprising and original to his readers (at least, this was what he hoped) was the third element Samir had injected into his paper. He'd added some of his own personal and cultural narrative — specifically, his fear of dogs and the *mépris* of Arabic and Islamic cultures towards dogs. And he had introduced this mention of his ethnicity at a time when Western academia was desperately looking for anything Arabic, and certainly Islamic, to integrate into their curriculum. In Samir's opinion, Western intellectuals had, for many years, undermined the grand Arabic and Islamic civilization for fear of being portrayed as sympathetic to the Palestinian cause or, even worse, for fear of being fatally accused of anti-Semitism. After the two towers collapsed in New York, Samir anticipated that, after the first phase of Western anger and bewilderment had passed, a new curiosity about Arabic and Islamic culture would emerge. Some reflection will come in the next phase, he said to himself. The Christian element of forgiveness and healing, cosmetic or not, persists in Western culture.

And so, Samir had structured his article around a cultural/geographical/historical trinity, with the images of dogs, devils and expelled creatures as its focal points. His article found a favourable reception with both the left and the right. Each pole found something to embrace. For those on the right, the article confirmed the cold-heartedness of a culture that couldn't tolerate even cute puppies and man's best friend (after God, of course). For those on the left, Samir's reference to an obscure, neglected, historically oppressed, colonial subject constituted an act of defiance that exposed academia's neglect of an important part of the world.

The head of the Faculty of Arts at Samir's university had been heard saying, approvingly: It is essential to give that culture a place in the artistic discourse at this time of collision between two worlds.

The night before he left for the airport, Samir sat in his favourite chair and ordered a Coke and a large pizza with pepperoni, not giving a shit if the meat was pork or dog. Waiting for the pizza, he embarked on a fantasy of fucking his cousin, Souad, back home in Jordan along with a few of her gaudy-looking girlfriends. It was always the same fantasy, more or less: It started with a drink in a hotel bar with his cousin and her friends, who brought him along as a chaperone to reassure their parents that their virginity would stay intact until a Muslim suitor, a rich Romeo, came along. Then his cousin's friends would decide to go to the house of one of the girls whose parents were away. Once there, his cousin would start drinking and ask him to dance with her, and in no time, Samir would strip all the girls naked, leaving only the flashy jewellery around their necks and the twenty-four-karat-gold earrings dangling below their chins while they howled like creatures with collars and chains.

After he ejaculated, Samir washed his hands, turned on the TV, opened a book and continued to wait for the pizza delivery. He was pleased by his ability to simultaneously read Kant, await food, watch wrestling, and contemplate the link between the three. In the end, the Kantian problem of transcendence and perception was solved through the secretion of saliva in his mouth upon hearing the doorbell rung by the pizza man.

The next day, on the flight, Samir complained to the flight attendant about not being able to properly watch his flat TV screen. He protested calmly, knowing that a Middle Eastern man's position on a plane these days was precarious, and his smile convinced the attendant that he indeed needed a change of seats because the angle of his chair forbade him from watching the Hollywood movie he longed to see. In fact, the flight attendant was so pleasant that he bumped Samir into first class, flirtatiously asking if he needed a little blanket to tuck himself in. Samir smiled but didn't bite. He watched his movie, and when the cabin lights dimmed, he pictured his cousin Souad in the seat adjacent to him with her brightly painted red toes and her fat ankles, pretending to be asleep, waiting for Samir's finger to crawl up her luscious, hummus-fed thighs.

At the airport in Japan, Samir was met by two Japanese organizers from the conference, who recognized him right away and led him to a waiting bus. The women smiled but did not bow, and one of them attempted a handshake that landed awkwardly on the back of Samir's hand because his fist was wrapped around the handle of his suitcase.

On the bus, Samir and his Japanese hosts chatted as people climbed aboard or exited. He noted a few Germans — or perhaps giant Dutch — in sandals, and a few Japanese people here and there, looking out the windows with the complacency of locals. Samir asked if Daido would attend the conference, and whether any of the well-known Japanese photographers of Daido's era and school would be there. Who was still alive and who was not? Were they still taking photographs, exhibiting abroad? Samir knew that Japanese writing about photography was filled with personal accounts, so he assumed that asking about the photographers' personal lives was acceptable.

One of the hosts, Mitsuko, was more knowledgeable than the other. She also looked much younger than her age, because, judging by her answers, she was a contemporary of Daido, Yutaka Takanashi and even Ken Domon, whom Samir had assumed must be dead by now. But Domon was evidently very much alive, although his militant philosophy on the "absolutely pure snapshot, absolutely unstaged" was, Samir mused, passé in this era of deconstruction and postmodernism.

After these inquiries, Samir gazed out the window and wondered if his cousin Souad would ever understand any of this. Her life was unexamined, he thought, and she was oblivious to history, geography and culture; hers was a small existence filled with morning coffees, petty gossip, the assessing of virgins while they waited for future husbands, providers of sperm and fancy cars parked behind metal gates, cars driven by chauffeurs who fucked the maids and chased dust with giant feather boas, swaying rhythmically like Cleopatra's servants over family cars, turning the metal shiny and bright. This was Samir's life's mystery: Why did these incestuous thoughts haunt him? Why was he obsessed with Souad, that empty-headed, made-up, Bedouin-royal-blood cousin who spent her days in some empty zone bordered by Al-Jazeera and CNN? Maybe it was because she'd been one of the few women around during Samir's sexual awakening and he'd never gotten over his first masturbation fantasies. Maybe he was subconsciously preserving an ancient tradition of inter-marriage. Or maybe it stemmed from his reading of Abu Nuwas, who, in his celebration of wine and male sexual free-dom, may have been the first Arab-Persian poet to write about masturbation (Samir now recalled his shocking verses, openly describing things that religion forbade). Or maybe it was the influence on Samir's younger, malleable mind of the pre-Islamic poet Imru' al-Qais, who, in one of his long and playful verses, had insinuated that he was fucking his cousin on the back of a camel.

Samir glanced at his hosts. Japanese women looked too fragile, too small, he thought. It was the roundness of Souad, her luscious exuberance, her almost repulsive glitter, that got him off. Perhaps that was why he had taken refuge in the aesthetic of the Japanese photographers. All that flagrant excess of makeup, colour and flesh was absent in their works.

Samir was taken to a small residence in Shinjuku. Small but good, Mitsuko said, and laughed.

Not American size, Samir said.

No. Small but good. Mitsuko laughed again.

Samir put his suitcase on the bed, which took up most of the space in the room. There was a small kitchenette, a tiny bathroom and a balcony that looked out on a construction site. The Japanese women bowed and left. Tomorrow, Mitsuko said on her way out, while the other woman smiled and retreated.

There was a TV hanging above the bed. At first, Samir searched for a porn channel or wrestling, but all he could find was the news and game shows with young men and women who giggled and shouted. Soon he was hungry and went downstairs. Vending machines were everywhere. Coffee, condoms, beer, food — all of these things could be retrieved from them. Without a map or a word of Japanese, he ventured into the street. He kept going in a straight line, and the farther he went, the busier the street got. He decided to go back to his room for fear of getting lost in the crowd. On the way back, he spotted a vegetable stand across from the hotel. He bought oranges and went upstairs. He opened all the drawers in the kitchenette but couldn't find a knife. He pierced an orange with his thumb, opened the balcony door and stood outside, chipping away bits of peel and leaving them on the edge.

After eating his oranges and showering, Samir lay on the bed and fell asleep. He woke up in the middle of the night, jet-lagged and thirsty. He poured a glass of water and grabbed the TV remote. Again he flipped through the channels, but still there was not even a glimpse of porn to find. He settled for a channel with English words written on the top left-hand side of the screen: *Healing Time*. Relaxing, soft music accompanied images of live rabbits hopping and grazing, moose strolling nonchalantly, birds gliding, rivers pouring off quiet cliffs. He was reminded of Al-Jahiz, the famous East African Arab intellectual who had lived in Baghdad during the Abassid Dynasty, and his book *Kitab al-Hayawan* (*Book of Animals*), a many-volume record of prose, poetry and proverbs describing hundreds of varieties of animals. Al-Jahiz had developed a theory about the influence of the environment on animals and men. In certain academic circles, the *Book of Animals* was considered a precursor to the theory of evolution, written centuries before Darwin.

Samir watched that channel until morning. The serenity was surprising, calming: it stopped everything. That night, Souad did not show up in his fantasies. Even the hoofs of the many herbivores that made sudden, quiet appearances on the screen did not remind him of his cousin's toes. Hours passed and Samir lay in bed, uttering not a word, not a sound. Just looking, as harmless animals appeared and disappeared against the greeneries of the passing world.

The next day, Samir gave his talk. When he was finished, some Japanese academics expressed reservations. Their questioning was polite but full of disapproval. The addition of Arabic culture to Samir's equation was met with skepticism. One academic objected that by placing too much emphasis on the context, Samir was implying that photography as such had no identity on its own. And to present Daido's work as a product of the master's own culture and religious traditions was to deny his independence, his effort to break with all ideologies and previous photographic traditions.

But, Samir replied, this was what Buddhism aspired to be: a transcendental, individualistic enlightenment that sought to break with all that had been previously learned and acquired.

A few Japanese heads nodded, and a man with a Leica took photographs of Samir without making a sound.

Afterwards, Samir went back to his room and lay in bed. He thought about his family. Eventually, he pulled a photograph out of his wallet, a group shot of the entire family. Souad stood next to him in the photo. She had placed her hand above his wrist.

The photo enraged him; its hypocrisy enraged him. The photo had been taken just before a cousin's wedding and everyone looked happy. But what had happened after this photograph had been shot was hideous. There had been a terrible fight, and the wedding had been cancelled. He started to tear the image slowly — first in half, then his father's side, with himself and Souad right in the middle, then his mother's side. Slowly, everyone lost a head or an arm and a leg.

Samir threw the pieces in the garbage. It was no use keeping a photo if a bad memory was attached to it.

A few days passed. Samir visited the fish market, some temples, a shrine. The tea ceremony he attended was very commercial, staged for tourists and naive Westerners who felt compelled to respect every foreign cup or ritual that landed in their lap. He took photos. He tried to find a way to get in touch with Daido but received polite and subtle refusals in answer to his inquiries. He was welcomed at a party at a Japanese professor's house with generous, polite, careful smiles and laughs. He found he couldn't remember anyone's name, but he was too embarrassed to pull out the business cards he'd been offered so that he might recall and address people properly. It might well have been the reason he'd been given these cards in the first place, but Samir felt that remembering — as Daido had said about photographs — should be a commemoration, not a recording.

After the party, he was driven back to his hotel by a Japanese artist who had smiled at him all evening until, at last, he'd approached her with a drink in his hand. In the car, she told Samir that his analysis of photography and Islam, a religion that forbade representation, could well be as offensive as his attempt to connect the meaning of Japanese photography to the ancient religion of Japan. If what you propose is true, then all meaning comes from history, and therefore our attempts to overcome the historical and social in our art have failed, and everything remains stagnant. Maybe in the Arab world that is the case, she added, but not in Japan.

Samir tried unsuccessfully to remember the woman's name. He stuck his hand in his pocket and surreptitiously pulled out a few business cards, but in the end, he just kissed her unexpectedly on the cheek. Then he opened the car door and wobbled his way, drunk, back up to his little room.

The next day, wind blew into the streets of Shinjuku. Samir walked through the rush of feet and solemn faces. He walked beneath large buildings and through traffic jams and under pedestrian bridges. He took photographs in strong winds and in back alleys. He ate, walked and held his camera against his waist. He took photographs all day. Finally, he entered a comic-book store with an Internet café to check his email. His sister had written to him. *Urgent. Father ... Call Saudi Arabia house immediately.*

Samir called his parents' home and heard wailing in the background.

His sister sobbed over the phone, saying only, Father, Father. Then she added, incoherently, He wanted to go home. He wanted to go back to his village in Palestine.

Souad came on the line. She sounded devastated. She told him the burial would take place that same day.

No, Samir thought, they won't wait. In Islamic ritual, the dead are wrapped in a simple piece of cloth and buried on the day of death, head towards the east. The ancient Arabs had never waited. They moved through the dunes and under the heat of the sun, leaving behind what couldn't be carried on their animals' backs.

His remaining days in Japan, Samir wandered aimlessly with his camera, taking photographs. He travelled farther each day, walking through the streets of villages, photographing trees, flowers, animals.

On his last day, he remembered something his father had once told him.

When his father's family had left their village in Palestine, the last thing his father had ever seen of that place was the road leading back to his house and a few stray dogs. We left, his father said, but the dogs stayed. And his father had looked behind at those strays and laughed.

MOTHER, MOTHER, MOTHER

THREE DAYS AGO, I received a call from my cousin saying that my mother had died. To tell the truth, I haven't visited her in my hometown of Beirut for the last five years. Between my family obligations and my work, it has been impossible to find time for such a trip.

I received the news with a certain indifference, treating it at first as a sudden, unexpected obstacle or complication of the kind I often encounter at work. I said to my crying cousin, briskly: I am on my way. I was not in mourning or feeling sentimental. I thought only of the details of the arrangements I had to make: informing my wife, booking my plane ticket, cancelling three or four appointments.

To my surprise, my wife was more emotional and wanted to come along, but I told her that her presence would only complicate things. And in fact, her presence already did, because she was offended at my composure. She naturally expected me to cry over the news of my mother's death; maybe she wanted to see me cry all the way to Beirut. But I did not cry then, or on the plane.

When I arrived in Lebanon, I went straight to the family home. It was only as the taxi pulled up to the building that I realized I had expected to see my mother there, in the doorway. And only then was I reoriented and transported to the past, to a life lived here and abandoned.

Mother, Mother, Mother, I shouted as I banged at my parents' bedroom door. She opened it wearing a flimsy, transparent robe that barely covered her thighs. My father lay under the quilt. I stood at the door and neither of my parents said a word. My mother did not go back to bed, and my father lit a cigarette, his lips transforming into a fuming locomotive hauling a chain of silent wagons, sliding doors open.

My mother, who never left the bedroom without a masquerade of blushes, shadows and lipsticks, sat at her mirror, unleashing the maelstrom of her elaborate disguise. Fat pencils approached her face with the precision of tools, followed by the cannon shot of powder puffs, pumped against her cheeks every day, usually twice or thrice, like prescribed medicine. I remember noticing that my mother's nipples were erect that day, and in hindsight, as I replay that scene from my childhood in my head, I wonder if this was caused by the dampness of the house or the earlier advances of my father's steaming lips on my mother's breasts.

I was beyond the age of suckling, and I had no siblings

following me to take over the mammalian extraction of liquid nourishment that a mother of our destructive species provides to future generations of this world. I just stepped inside the room and stood at a distance behind her, looking at myself in her mirror. After a while, I moved closer, and as I grew bigger in my mother's eyes, I reached for her brush, combed my hair, then grabbed her lipstick. My mother smiled, but my father frowned and held out his hand to retrieve the medicine. I went and stood next to his pillow, facing his bare chest, as he took the brush from my child's hand. He asked me to close my eyes and repeat after him:

"I, the child of my father and mother, will not grow up to become a hairdresser, nor ever paste makeup on my face, or dance onstage in the presence of other men . . . Repeat after me," he said.

And I did repeat.

"And I, the child and the man to be, will not wear high heels or a dress and will not look in the mirror at my reflection," my father said.

To my reflection, I repeated, "I will only look at myself when shaving for a funeral and when fixing my wedding tie." As I concluded, I heard my mother's loud laugh. She waved a pencil away from the mirror and over the arch of her eye.

As I made my way out of the room, my mother held me and showered me with a mixture of French and Arabic words, their sound and affection colliding. "Come over here and don't listen to your father, he is so old-fashioned and *il est fou* ... Come, let me comb your hair, and here, I will even put some lipstick on your cheeks."

I grabbed the brush once more and started to comb my mother's hair, and she laughed her exuberant laugh and asked her hairdresser for a kiss. Then she pushed me into her bosom and my lips landed on the space between her breasts.

My mother was a beauty who loved the company of the mirrors that were forbidden to me. She was a master of disguise. She was able to live at various altitudes, in different terrains and cities; she presented her flamboyant self to everyone and everything, even the birds, the goats and the villagers. She was also good at managing maids and the nobility, the clergy and doctors. All this she learned from examining herself in the mirror. All was made known to her through the reflection of the self. Her daily consultation with the mirror even made it possible for her to become a society hostess, at ease among the waving batons of long, thin cigarettes that glowed throughout prolonged nights of drinking and black spades flashing in fanning decks of cards. A versatile chameleon she was, my mother, colourful, stern but flexible, capable of modulating, in any moment, charm, affection and wrath. She could turn pious, sinking to her suddenly gelatinous knees in the presence of the devout; rising and turning away, she was able to sprout high, pointy heels and grow leather shoes from the tips of her toes; and she claimed to have ascended, more than once, in her diminutive skirts, the decadent heights of Beirut's most famous dancing clubs. She was also a magazine reader, the commander of domestic order, a gregarious socialite — and a tragic tear-shedder on the occasional nights when she blamed the mirror for its treacherous reflection of decaying looks.

Once, when our young maid, Nabila, came out of the shower, my mother asked her to stand naked beside her so that they could face the mirror together and compare how tall they were, the colour of their hair, the clarity of their skin. And so Nabila shivered next to my mother, her untrimmed pubic hair advancing in black abundance towards the lower side of the mirror. Bewildered and not knowing where to look, Nabila closed her eyes and waited. My mother gathered Nabila's hair and raised it off her neck, and asked Nabila to open her eyes and look at the mirror. Then my mother released Nabila's hair and lifted her own. She instructed Nabila to turn around, made her put on a pair of heels, and finally ordered her to put her clothes back on and return to the kitchen.

My mother mumbled, "The little girl is a woman now. She won't be staying with us for long."

And then my mother reclaimed the mirror's space for herself, and with her fingers, she stretched her face and pushed it towards the glass. She touched her nose, the bottom of her eyelids, and pointed her index finger at her thighs.

"Look what childbirth did to your mother," she said, before asking me to leave. I resisted for fear that her sadness might glue her to that glass window that mimics everything we do and lip-syncs all the words we say. But I was reassured when she pulled out the powder puff, made it quiver in the air and started the daily process of colouring herself in. I gave her back her hairbrush and left, looking for the maid, for company and for food.

Our maid Nabila was young, and her hair was long and straight and dark and often anointed with oil, and she had sad, mischievous, beautiful eyes. My father never acknowledged her presence except to ask her to find his silky scarf or to bring him his daily doses of cigarettes and food, and my mother hardly communicated with her either, except about holiday preparations or lavish dinner parties that she threw for the opulent, pretentious couples of her social circle. Nabila slept in the back room behind the kitchen and walked me to school every day. She was older than me, illiterate but perceptive, quiet but courageous. She would often ask me about school and my teachers with a large, curious smile on her face. And in time, she confided in me her desire to read and go to school, to join all these kids in uniforms. It was the thing she wanted most in life, she said. So I taught her the alphabet and how to count numbers. On our daily walks, she memorized the Arabic alphabet and was able to associate letter shapes with their sounds. Then, one evening, my mother caught her reading in the back room. My mother asked what she was doing, and Nabila said that she was looking at the pictures.

My mother frowned and asked her in dismay, "And where did you get the magazine from?"

"From your room, Madame," Nabila answered in a bashful, shameful whisper.

My mother snatched the magazine from the young maid's hand, slapped her, turned off the lights in her room and instructed her to go to sleep.

When my mother went away on her card nights, and my father was busy with his friends, Nabila would ask me to come to her room. She would lie down in her underwear and proudly read to me. We played a game where every time she mispronounced a word, she would ask me to pinch her inner thighs. She would close her eyes and wait for my fingers to touch her legs and grasp the right amount of flesh, and I would pinch her with my index finger and thumb. Then she would sigh and hold my hand for a while between her round thighs and squeeze it until I pulled my hand back for fear of losing my fingers in an abyss of lava and pain. After a few of these mispronunciations and reading mistakes, she would lay her own hands on her pubis and close her eyes, remind me to keep our secret, and ask me to leave her alone.

Every summer, right after the school year was over and the Persian carpets in every household had been slapped and dusted away on city roofs, my mother would invite two villagers to our house and order Nabila to pack our clothing into brown leather suitcases. Some of our furniture was then loaded onto the villagers' truck and off we went in my father's car to the mountains, rolling along behind our tables and chairs to a village named after a local monastery that had existed, it seemed, forever, or at least long before our time. In the car, my father would play the radio and my mother would look in the rear-view mirror and give orders to Nabila to close the back window, or cover me with a blanket, or feed me from the bag of food that accompanied us.

The village in the Lebanese mountains was perched very high above the seashore. To reach it, we had to take the familiar serpentine road that ran along the edge of cliffs. Huge blocks of stone filled the valleys and marked the summits, sometimes humbled into man-made stairs that I often imbued with mythical purpose. Giants, I would say to myself, must have lived here once and used these steps to climb to the peak to gather snow, and then rolled the stones back down to the shore, where they crushed the fish in the sea.

The mountains were populated by what my father, with a hint of mockery and a sense of his superiority, called the Pale Tribes. My father felt a mixture of dismay and pride before these Noble Savages, as he would call them — employing this expression to tease my francophone mother. I took pride in my father's high rank, his condescending attitude and his sophisticated manner of driving, one hand dangling out the window. As we drove our way along these ominous roads, from the back seat, I followed the trail of smoke from his cigarette, distinct in its elegance and thinness from the fumes of trucks and other cars and burning wood and the various other fires of this world. I so admired my father's confidence, his quiet manner and his debonair looks: his trim moustache, his silk scarf around his neck, his hair well combed, his face closely shaved — done without once glancing in a mirror, because my father and I, twice or even three times a week, visited the neighbourhood barber.

When we arrived in the village, my mother would open the door of our old house there with her large, bulky key. The green wooden ancestral door would issue an incomprehensible utterance. The house was in the middle of the village, a stone building with three arched windows in the front and a roof of red European tile in a triangular shape. The jasmine on the balcony, and view of the meadows beyond, never impressed my father, an urbanite and lover of bright lights and car exhausts. But once upon a time, before I came into being, my father must have considered a country life. He and his barber had gone on a hunting trip, and it was then that my father saw my mother for the first time. She was wearing a school uniform and walking in the company of nuns in that little village. My father had a car and an expensive hunting rifle, and he dressed in the manner of colonial hunters, his feet dominating the ground in leather boots that reached to the tops of his knees and what seemed to be the end of his puffy plus-fours.

In the company of the barber — who acted as his servant, even dressing like one — my father, the well-groomed hunter, strode through the village with dead birds hanging from his waist belt and bouncing off his thighs. Both men cradled their rifles in their arms and fluttered their own urban feathers. There was a café in the village centre, with a little stream running through it, cutting it in half. My father sat at a table under the pine trees and waited. When the owner appeared, he asked my father about the hunt and the mark of his rifle, and my father introduced himself; all his life, he never missed the chance to mention his family name or where he came from. His lineage and his money and the reputation of his family commanded immediate respect in our feudal and pious society.

After eating and paying the owner and leaving him a handsome tip, and without fear or embarrassment, my father inquired about my mother, the pretty girl he had seen while hunting. Then he and his companion — the barber with the sharp nose and trail of cheap perfume and traces of clients' hair upon his shoulders — went straight to the convent school. There, fearless, arrogant and rich, my father stood in the school's archway and waited for the Mother Superior.

When she arrived, he introduced himself and asked for the girl by the name of Rafka.

"Come next year," Mother Superior said, "after she finishes her schooling. The girl is a ward of the convent, but after next year, she will be on her own."

My father said that he would like to meet Rafka right away.

The nun shook her head. The girl was the convent's responsibility and would be released into her uncle's care in a year's time. So, my father prolonged his stay in the village. He came every day to the school and stood out front, beside his large car. He showed off his wealth and dangled his collection of guns and dead birds, while the barber slept in the front seat with a hat over his face.

And one summer's day, my mother walked out of the school, past the nuns' gate, and without a bag or a penny, climbed into the back seat of my father's car and left with the barber and the rich man. My parents eloped to a church in the city, with the sister of the presiding priest as maid of honour and the barber as best man.

My mother had been orphaned at an early age. After the death of her parents, she had inherited the house in the village and was assigned to the custody of her uncle, a priest who often travelled to the Nordic countries to call together what was left of his parish, most of whom had emigrated to Sweden for work. This uncle put my mother in the convent to be raised by the nuns, under his distant watch.

The villagers still remembered my mother and loved her. Immediately upon arriving in the village, my mother would walk towards the neighbours, shouting in such an uncharacteristic way that my father would wince and imitate her rustic accent, and lean into my hair and whisper in my ear, "Once a bumpkin, always a bumpkin." Amid this parade of affection and lurid tribal greetings, my father would keep his distance from the primitive debauchery of love and blood relations, avoiding the tears of joy. He would light a cigarette and watch as the villagers kissed my mother's cheeks, held her hands and carried her bags. Then, all of a sudden, my turn would come, and I'd experience the welcoming licks applied to lost wolves upon their return to the pack. Plump distant aunts and fat cousins would appear from behind tall stones and pine trees to kiss me on the forehead and cheeks, leaving me sedated by their long, snail-like saliva traces. In their slow drawls, they would ask me about the city. The women smelled of the kitchen, of dough especially, and their aprons were stained by the prints of their children's dirty hands and faces. They greeted my father from afar, with a mixture of aloofness and pride, for they could now lay claim to an association with our good lineage and his name. My father would bestow on everyone a little, proud smile before he walked back towards the car, looking at his watch as if hoping for an immediate departure back to the city and away from this primitive herd.

But I felt safe among these mountains and villagers. There

was no reflection but the sky — no glass, no windows and no little mirror for me to appear in or be seen by. I played with the village kids and swung from the trees and lost myself between meadows and the locusts and the chameleons and the domesticated beasts. I ran with my distant cousins from dawn until night while my mother hosted her distant relatives, the villagers, on her balcony and cooked in a commune of women with round, bulky calves and pudgy, rosy cheeks.

When my father finally went back to the city to take care of matters of wealth and his estate, my mother would at first sit in the kitchen and cry. And then she would neglect her appearance and disregard the old mirrors and her collection of brushes and powders — and within a few days, she would turn back into the villager she had been before my father rescued and moulded her into an urbanite lover of high society.

After the summer ended, we returned to the city.

Soon after this, I realized that my game of thigh pinching with Nabila had stopped. She no longer needed my linguistic instruction, and my ignorance in matters of sexual fulfillment must have ceased to be satisfactory to her. I could not compete with the French actors who left behind the pages of magazines every night and slipped into her tiny bed behind the kitchen and looked her in the eyes and asked her to open her thighs and enter the glamorous society of crowds wrapped in fox furs and low-cut dresses.

Instead, when my parents were out for their casino nights or to see a play, Nabila would borrow a dress from my mother's closet and put it on, and convince me to wear heels and a wig. We would sit and converse in French while we smoked and drank — juice, not alcohol — stuffing ourselves with sweets and talk of handsome men. Nabila closely observed my mother's manners and listened to my parents' snooty friends confabulate in French while she, Nabila, swept the floor and cleaned the toilet after the guests' filthy defecations and humiliating fluids. The maid soon baffled my mother, even scared her, with her understanding of French conversation. When my mother and her lady friends exchanged banalities and superficial assessments of their material acquisitions and inconsequential bourgeois existence, an exhalation of *Ah, j'ai soif* was immediately met by a glass of water from Nabila — and my mother would boast of her maid who could understand French, insinuating that French was the language of choice in the household. And so Nabila became both a source of bewilderment and a threat to my mother. And afterwards, the maid would be subjected to curfews and accusatory inquiries about her education and the various books found under her bed. My mother even checked Nabila's underwear for stains indicating desire. When she did these things, she became her own Mother Superior, turning from society lady into an old nun with unshaved armpits and hairy legs. She brought to that little room behind the kitchen the judgment of monasteries, with their disdain for bodily pleasures and concealed thoughts of love.

But Nabila stood her ground. She threatened my mother, saying that with one phone call to her father, who was a Syrian soldier, she would be rescued, because her father could not bear the sound of one little teardrop falling from her eyes. In this way, Nabila reminded my mother that her people were the rulers of this land now.

When the war started, my father bought a new handgun and walked with it hanging from his hip inside a leather pouch. Oh, what a stroke of luck this war was for my father. With his inheritance, his lineage, and armed with his secret-society pin on his expensive tweed jacket, his appearance of nobility was complete. A warrior at last! A warrior at last! A prince with arms in one hand and precious sapphire beads in the other, he walked the streets and showed off his new steel piece and pushed his stones in between his thumb and forefinger.

But when the first bombs landed in our neighbourhood, my father realized the magnitude of rockets and their devastating effect, their lethal capacity to turn walls the colour of flesh and blood. After the first bombs, my father's theatrical play crumbled and, for the first time in his life, he felt fear for his family and understood the devastating meaning of a gun barrel. He decided to drive us back to the safety of my mother's village.

In the car, my mother had a quarrel with my father. "How can you leave us there and go back to the war?" she asked in tears. "There is killing, Joseph . . ."

"The house," he said. "Someone has to stay in the house . . . Obligations . . . business . . ." I heard him say something about a bank, and something about the honour of a nation.

My mother answered, "Your place is here with us. We have a house in the village. The bank can wait."

But my father hated the village. He preferred death to boredom and petty gossip, preferred death to the absence of an appreciative neighbourhood audience, urban spectators, connoisseurs who could truly assess his new movie-star outfit, his daily parade of ties, hats and jackets, and his matador walk through the imagined applause of the arena. His pride wouldn't allow him to leave the war and hide. His presence among the fighters and the war criminals was essential for morale — or so he thought. If the gentry leave the war, who will remain to make it colourful and make the fighting worthwhile?

Mother cried all the way to the village, burying her face in my father's handkerchief. And Nabila — upon seeing my sadness, or maybe simply resenting my mother's self-indulgence — held my hand in the back seat and directed it towards her warm thighs and the edge of her pubis. In the cold elevation of the mountains and enveloping fog, I felt concealed by the warm secretions between her thighs, her untrimmed, undomesticated pubic hair liberated from the wide cotton underwear that slowly turned into damp cloth while she directed my finger in small rotations, rhythmic pressures. The car zigzagged above tiny roads while she persistently pushed my index further inside and beyond the elastic band of her shorts. But when my mother suddenly screamed at my father, entreating him not to go back, I hastily withdrew my hand and repositioned my index finger below my nostrils. I caught a faint whiff of urine and a musky, moist fragrance that has stayed with me for the rest of my life, and which so often, through the rest of my adolescence and adulthood, I have craved.

Our village house was open, but the villagers were less welcoming and more apprehensive this time, worried and wanting to know about the war. Tentatively, one by one, they approached my father, calling him *ustaz* and quietly inquiring about the situation in the city. My father replied with few words, repeating things he had heard in the news or read in the paper. And he described our journey and how he had taken certain roads to avoid snipers and conflict zones. He sounded like a hero, or perhaps a careless madman, driving his family through dangerous terrain. One woman said to him, "Our Holy Mother must have protected you on your way," and my father smiled the sarcastic smile of a skeptic and a heathen.

But soon after this came news of massacres. Only a few villagers showed off their guns and hunting rifles now.

"We will protect ourselves if those Muslims come," one villager, a distant relative of my mother, said with pride, an old rifle in his hand.

Towards dusk that day, my father went out in the company of several other men and shot his gun, aiming at a bottle above a rock. Then he returned to the city.

Nabila felt neglected in the village. I no longer needed her games or her food. I became a feral child in those high mountains. I would roam the hills and play, and roam and play, hour after hour.

One evening, after I came back from a long day of adventures, I saw Nabila walking towards me. She stopped and showed me the bruises on her face.

"Look," she said. "This is what your mother did."

A few days later, a man arrived in a car with a Syrian licence plate. He got out, walked to our house, and introduced himself as an officer in the Syrian army and Nabila's father. Our maid had already packed her clothes and was ready. She asked my mother for the rest of her salary, hopped up into her father's car and left without bidding me farewell.

My mother, affecting an air of indifference, looked at herself in the mirror and said, "She is a grown woman now and she had to go."

On their way back to the city, Nabila and her father were stopped at a checkpoint. The militia saw the Syrian licence plate and asked for ID. Nabila spoke to them in French, but to no avail. Her father was asked to step out of the vehicle and taken at gunpoint to the side of the road. Nabila heard a shot and ran towards the sound. Her father was lying on the pebbled ground, blood coming out of the back of his head.

Shortly after, a man called my father, who was still in the city, and asked him to come to the militia headquarters. He said that a French-speaking woman named Nabila was in their custody; she had given his name and number, and he needed to come and identify her.

My father drove to the headquarters and found Nabila in a small underground room where she was being held alone. She was curled up in a corner like a mothball. When she saw my father, she stood up, laughed hysterically and said to him, *"Ah, te voilà, mon chouchou. On va au restaurant ou au cinéma?"*

The militia released Nabila into my father's custody, and in response to her entreaty, he promised the maid that he would drive her to the Syrian border. The militia advised him not to, but my father was seen getting into his car with Nabila, taking off his silky scarf and removing his jacket. He rolled up his sleeves and drove in the direction of Syria. And that was the last we ever heard of him.

The door was open, and hearing voices in the hallway, I entered my old house. Many people dressed in black turned their faces towards me, and my cousin, looking much older than I remembered, hurried over and kissed me. The mourners — my mother's loyal neighbours — stood and waited in turn to offer condolences.

With a rush of memory, I recalled how, in the years before I left for good, my mother had waited at the front window of this house, humming to herself. She would wake up in the morning and fix her hair, then disappear and occupy the bathroom for a while. Then she would hop between mirrors and fix her hair again and paint her face. For a long time after my father's disappearance, her obsession with her looks increased. She shaved her eyebrows and drew two black lines in the shape of swords above her eyes; the powder on her cheeks was applied so as to form perfect red balls like the noses of circus clowns. And like a magician or clairvoyant, she said aloud to herself every move she was about to make: "And now Rafka does the dishes before her husband comes back from his trip with the maid. And now Rafka checks on the maid and prepares for the evening's outing."

During those last years, my mother never went outside the house, relying instead on the neighbours now crowded around me. She remained inside for fear that the telephone might ring, that my father would be on the other end of the line, asking her to pick up his suit from the cleaner's or get ready for a night out. She gave orders to invisible maids and had long conversations with the ghosts of society ladies around her card table. And just before I left for good, when the bombs started to fall again and I knocked on her bedroom door and cried out desperately for her — *Mother, Mother, Mother* — she did not answer. I found her in the maid's room, curled on the little bed there, wrapped in our family's sorrow and all my unshed tears.

THE WHISTLE

WHEN I WAS SIXTEEN, I convinced my cousin to chase falling bombs in the streets of Beirut with me. The objective was to get a photograph of a bomb before it reached the ground or landed on a building, on a car, on a street — before it caused death and mayhem. The camera was his, but we shared its use. The car we drove in pursuit of falling bombs was my father's. Our attempts to capture these images never produced anything. We sent the film off for development, but all we got back were photographs of blue skies, clouds, roads and the tops of buildings.

The decisive moment — to use Henri Cartier-Bresson's famous expression — was not determined by our visual anticipation of what would come into the frame of the camera; our moment was decided by the sound of the bomb's whistle. My cousin and I stood on highways, or in alleys between buildings, aiming our lens towards the trajectory of whistles.

Eventually, I left Beirut, and twenty years later, on a visit to that Mediterranean city, I reminded my cousin of our madness years ago, running after falling bombs. He nodded and said,

It's a miracle that we are still alive. Miracles, I said, do not exist. They do, he said, and the proof is that we are here and alive, in spite of people's stupidity and the terror we endured. You believed in miracles back then, he reminded me.

I had spent all my savings on that last trip to Lebanon and had no job to fall back on. Upon my return to Montreal, I stayed in bed for weeks, unable to move. I began to contemplate suicide.

Then one day, suddenly, I decided to get up. I walked from my Côte-des-Neiges apartment to a government clinic. The social worker, Marc, who interviewed me there happened to be an acquaintance from my university days. We had both completed degrees in fine arts and, like the majority of people with such qualifications, found it hard to get a job afterwards. Marc went back to college and finished a degree in social work, while I drifted for a while, holding many small, inconsequential jobs. In class, Marc had always seemed arrogant, with an air of superiority. He was well-read and eloquent but had no talent as an artist. He seduced men and women equally. His critique of people's artwork was very perceptive and analytical, but he was always dismissive.

Now, in the clinic, Marc asked me what method of suicide I was considering.

A bullet, I said.

A bullet from a gun? he asked.

Yes, I replied.

You would be the person to be pulling the trigger?

Yes.

Can you imagine where you would be standing?

On the balcony.

And you would be looking in which direction? he asked.

At the sky, I guess.

And what part of your body would you aim at?

This interrogation lasted for a while, seemingly to assess the seriousness of my intention. Then Marc asked me what I had been doing before I had thought of ending my life.

I had just come back from a visit to Beirut, I replied.

You could well be suffering post-traumatic stress, he said. Then quickly added, But that has to be determined by a psychologist. I am here to gauge what channels and options are open to you. Is there anything in particular that happened in Beirut that you would like to discuss?

Nothing in particular, I said. I met with the family.

Anything that sticks in your memory from those meetings? he said.

I had a few dinners with family members and old friends. I visited a cousin who was a childhood friend.

What did you talk about?

We were reminiscing about when I was sixteen, and we'd carried his camera around with the intention of capturing the image of a falling bomb.

And did you capture it? Marc asked.

No, we never did.

And why do you think you wanted to capture the image of a bomb in a photograph?

Death, I said. And I laughed at the vagueness of my answer.

It's no laughing matter, Marc said, unsmiling. Anyhow, photography is always about death, he added.

Barthes, *Camera Lucida*, I said, and we both smiled, having read the same books in university.

You were not afraid? he asked me.

No, I said.

Did you think of it as an act of suicide back then?

No, I said. I wouldn't have brought my cousin with me, I guess, if that was my intention.

So suicide is a private matter to you?

Yes, I said. I think it should be. Otherwise, it's murder or an intention to harm.

And what would you have done with the photograph, if you'd happened to capture a bomb falling from the sky?

It would have been a trophy, I said. Undeniably a rare image.

Your interest in image making started in your youth, then? Marc asked.

Yes.

But the camera itself was your cousin's?

Yes, but we shared it. And the car we drove on our mission was my father's.

Marc paused and looked intently at me. Then he said, Listen, this is our option: I have to assign you to a specialist to further assess your situation.

And then? I asked.

The psychologist will determine what to do next.

And what would that be, hypothetically? I said.

Anything from medical treatment to hospitalization.

But I have never actually owned a gun — or a bullet for that matter. Firing it is entirely hypothetical, I said.

The process is out of our hands now, he said, and stretched back in his revolving chair. What did you expect from your visit here?

To talk things over, I said. Not to be potentially incarcerated.

Well, I am curious, Marc continued. What is your cousin's situation now?

He stayed in Beirut. In fact, he never left home.

And what has he been doing with his life for the past twenty years since chasing the bombs?

Nothing. He continuously whistles. It's irritating. And he has stayed living at home ever since we were kids. Never got a job, he borrowed money, and he lives at his parents' house with his sister, who provides for him from her secretarial job.

Was he the one driving the car when you chased bombs?

No, I did the driving.

Was he the one who took the photographs?

No, I did.

There was a pause, and Marc and I looked into each other's eyes.

He didn't come with you of his own free will, did he? Marc asked. You dragged him along. You forced him. And he must have been terrified. He didn't want to die.

I said nothing.

Well? Did he come with you of his own volition? Marc repeated.

No, I said, defiant now.

What did you do to him, to get him to go along?

I called him a coward, I said. I stood up to walk towards the door.

And what else did you tell him? insisted Marc quietly. He waited a long moment for my answer.

I told him if he had faith, nothing would ever happen to him.

And precisely nothing has ever happened to him since, Marc said. He stood up then, too, and accompanied me to the door.

No need, I said. I can find my way out.

That is still to be seen, said Marc.

I strode away and down the corridor, aware he was watching me, as dismissive as the critic he'd once aspired to be. Then I heard him turn and close the door firmly behind me.

THE FATE OF THE SON

OF THE MAN ON THE HORSE

Photographs are traces of apparitions.

— Unknown

SOPHIA LOREN SURPRISED EVERYONE when, on her visit to the city of Montreal in 1970, she stopped outside a residential block on Saint-Laurent Boulevard in Little Italy, took the stairs to the second floor, arrived at unemployed photographer Giuseppe Cassina's tiny apartment, went inside, pushing back her entourage, and, to the amazement of the paparazzi and fans trailing behind her, locked the door, before — perhaps needlessly — introducing herself.

Sophia Loren, celebrated in both Hollywood and Europe, then asked the photographer if his mother was home. Confused, Giuseppe informed her that his mother had died — a year ago to the day, in fact. And then he stood there in his pyjamas before glamour personified, listening to journalists shout Sophia Loren's name and bang at the door of the small flat that, until her passing, he had shared with his mother, even though he was thirty-eight.

Giuseppe was at his worst in that moment: mourning his mother but unable to afford flowers to lay on her grave. Sophia Loren, with her broad smile and famous figure towering over him, handed Giuseppe a fancy envelope manufactured far away, elsewhere, not in this distant northern city where stationery and even the standard dimensions of photographs were different from what he now held in his hand. He offered the actress a cup of tea, and she laughed and said, cryptically, Had you known, you would have spent your life being served. Giuseppe could not understand why she was there, or what she meant, so he simply held the envelope in one hand and watched as the actress carefully applied some makeup, consulting a small oval mirror that she pulled from her designer handbag, before opening the door to face the screaming cluster of journalists who now retreated down the bleak and narrow stairs that reeked of damp winter shoes and, despite the bakery below, poverty.

Alone once more, Giuseppe placed the envelope on his mother's kitchen table and wondered at the absurdity of what had just happened — surely a farce, some big mistake. He finished his coffee, contemplating how best to ask the baker for money. He had sold his camera months ago, and what little money his mother had left him had been spent on a tie and new socks to wear to her funeral.

Giuseppe had learned the photographic craft by working as an assistant to a Hungarian Jewish photographer named

Laszlo, who had sympathized with his mother's irreligious nature. His mother, meanwhile, had worked at the bakery downstairs, although only part-time in later years. His mother's affair with the baker had never been an issue for Giuseppe. As a kid, he'd often encountered the baker, who had a long, droopy moustache and would offer him cakes and, on occasion, ruffle his hair. With time, he grew to associate his mother's good moods, her singing of old Italian songs, with traces of flour and the scent of male sweat in her bed. Bread and sweets were always to be found in the apartment in abundance when he was a boy, and sometimes wine too, which would make his mother reach for her child, hold him tight and cry her drunkenness away.

He stepped downstairs in his torn coat, rehearsing the humiliation of begging from the baker, anticipating another lecture on getting his life together, on how at his age — at this late stage, in other words — he should consider giving up his illusions, his delusions (a photographer with no camera!), and settle down, find himself a secure job at last . . .

But as soon as Giuseppe reached the street, he was surrounded by a crowd of inquisitive journalists and neighbourhood men wearing big smiles, some cheering, some leering, some thrusting their hips, some calling him not Cassina but Casanova, some chanting the name "Sophia Loren," pointing to their chests in semicircle gestures and whispering obscenities. It was as if the whole neighbourhood was patting him on the back while journalists' eyes followed him and women from their windows called to him. Only the baker stood outside his tired shopfront, looking thoughtful all the while.

When at last there was a moment of calm in the commotion, Giuseppe was asked by a reporter about his connection to Sophia Loren. And in defiance of his usually shy, stuttering self, in a moment of inspiration and courage, he replied, She stood there and asked me to take her photograph.

Having escaped the crowd, Giuseppe headed over to the cemetery, hoping his new-found fame would compensate for his lack of flowers. He recalled how feisty his mother was. What would she have made of Sophia Loren? Whenever his mother had encountered other made-up women, gaudy and flashily ornamental, she would turn into a challenging, even mocking, working-class rebel. He could see her now, bossing the actress around, shaking her flour-coughing apron and her dough-coated cook's fingers threateningly — and then he remembered the envelope on the table at home, the paper that had touched the actress's hands. He realized he still had no idea why she had asked him about his mother. Perhaps she is a distant relative, he murmured to himself, though this seemed implausible.

After all the years of living with his mother's reserve, he was content not to query the mysteries of her past too deeply.

The actress's appearance had been chaotic and brief, and all he remembered clearly now was the envelope and the lingering perfume that had masked the apartment's pungent odour, a miasma perpetually trapped between the narrow walls without windows, no purifying sun rays, except for a square opening in the kitchen that gave onto the alley of his childhood, a street still occupied by the long shadows of the ghosts of the Babacci kids and their bullying ways. He felt ashamed that he had not appreciated, in the moment, Sophia Loren's beauty – a beauty the swarm that had followed her and later buzzed about him on the street confirmed.

On his way back home from the cemetery, he made a detour.

Later, opening the envelope, he found a large number of American dollars, a series of photographs of a village he didn't recognize, a letter scrawled in handwritten Italian – a language he was able to converse in but not read – and an eight-by-ten photograph, a headshot of the actress, autographed, and dedicated on the back to his mother, "With love and solidarity, Sophia."

For a time, the neighbourhood men and women would stop Giuseppe and ask to see the photo he had taken of the great Italian actress Sophia Loren. The joke was that he'd forgotten to load his film, or that he'd been so nervous he had grabbed his shoes instead of his camera, or that he'd stuttered and shook in his usual way, which had caused the photograph to blur.

One morning, Giuseppe walked to a photography store and bought a new camera, a tripod and two tungsten lights. He set up the lamps and laid the black-and-white photo of the actress on the table. He examined her smile for a moment, looking for a connection, a family resemblance — and once again concluded that it was unlikely. His mother was short and round, and the great Italian actress Sophia Loren was neither.

He carefully photographed the original image that had once been tucked in the envelope alongside the Italian letter and the American dollars. Then he rented a darkroom, developed the film, printed the negative and reproduced a copy of the portrait. He made multiple copies, framing and hanging one at the entrance of the building for all the world to see, along with a sign with his name and profession on it. Naturally, the autograph and the dedication to his mother were not reproduced in his copies, as that would have exposed the fact that he hadn't photographed the great Italian actress himself.

Soon Giuseppe became a celebrity in the neighbourhood, a hitherto hidden talent, a little gem who had lived among others in silence and humility, a favourite of the Hollywood set, photographer to the stars. Soon he was approached to take beauty portraits. "Make me look like her," the ladies would instruct Giuseppe Cassina, photographer extraordinaire, giggling with excitement.

One morning, the priest who had buried Giuseppe's mother knocked at his door, having examined the portrait of the celebrity who had unexpectedly visited this corner of Montreal. He entered the apartment to explore the holy site where the miraculous apparition, the great Italian actress Sophia Loren, had materialized, here in the cold north, transfiguring Giuseppe, the former outcast.

The priest sat on a chair, while Giuseppe busily fixed his new tie in a large mirror on the wall.

My child, the priest said, your mother never believed in the Lord. She was a Communist, and that's why I was severe at the time of her burial.

His mother had been well-known for her hate of religiosities and her antagonism towards the Church, which she had forbade her son to enter. Her corpse had lain in the morgue for a few days, while Giuseppe had waited for the Church to decide whether to permit her burial in the cemetery. The Church of the Madonna della Difesa had finally agreed to provide a rectangular slice of its earth but refused Giuseppe's mother a spot in heaven, and indeed no prayers were said to save her soul.

I remember, continued the priest, when you were little . . . I feared for your soul and asked your mother many times to bring you to be baptized, but she wouldn't hear of it. And you,

I believe, have never been inside our church, the most beautiful in Montreal and the entire country, I dare say. Yes, we have a bad reputation because of that fresco, but now we can't do anything about it. Some of our congregation were even placed in internment camps during the war in Europe. Imagine that, here in Canada. But what is past is past. And a church is a place of worship, after all. Why don't you come and visit, and take in its beauty and experience its tranquility and contemplate your soul? The Lord loves all his children, just like I love you, my son. And if you do choose to visit, it is conceivable that the relationship might be beneficial to both of us. Now that God has bestowed on you this great artistic talent and sent you a sign from Rome to rescue you from sin and poverty, I hope you will permit me to offer you something more.

What *more*? Giuseppe said.

My son, our congregation needs talent like yours. We need photos of baptisms, first communions, marriages, and our annual Easter parade. And our community can pay you well, what you deserve, for your photographs. Do you accept Jesus, my son?

Yes, said Giuseppe casually, brushing and admiring his new Italian patent leather shoes.

Okay, good. Come on Sunday. The priest held Giuseppe's shoulders and looked into his eyes. You have an air of familiarity, my son, as if I encounter you daily, the priest concluded, before making his way down the dark stairs.

The following Sunday, Giuseppe wore his new suit and strolled into the church that he had walked by so many times in his life but had never dared enter. The chancel, and the large circle of stained glass in the middle of the square edifice, and the bell tower — all of these reminded him of his obedience to his mother's edict that he should never set foot in here. But now that she was dead, he had found the courage to disobey — something he had never dared do before, neither as a child nor as a young man.

He saw many familiar faces from the neighbourhood. Women with lace scarves loosely settled atop their puffed hair had left behind their monotonous weekday housedresses — left them hanging on bathroom doors or on the corner posts of single beds that their husbands nevertheless conquered at night after the kids fell asleep — and here they stood, before the flamboyance of the altar, scattered between parallel rows of pews as regimental in their horizontal exactitude as note-books, some kneeling beside men, exposing the soles of their shoes, some frowning and holding their restless children by their arms. Little girls stood stupefied in bell-shaped dresses, and little boys looked like small facsimiles of their fathers, perhaps wondering if they too could be suspended from the roof like the Jesus floating above them in his fluttering toga. Italian builders, stonemasons and groundskeepers stood in their Sunday clothes, their broad shoulders like the bases of tri-angles, which put Giuseppe in mind of secret-society symbols, inverted pyramids housing the Eye of Providence. He spotted the Babacci brothers, grown older like him, and their wives, who borrowed their demeanours from their mothers, along with austere looks, cylindrical calves and scrutinizing eyes. When Angela Babacci saw Giuseppe a few rows back, she whispered in her husband Felice's ear, causing him to turn abruptly, staring with the same childhood expression, his twitching eyes signalling the ensuing extortion of sweets and money. And then slowly the benches between them seemed to disappear, filled by the faithful who were squeezing themselves along rows of wood grown as black as mould, black as donjons.

The intense smell of his fellow parishioners' perfume was nauseating to Giuseppe, as were the screams of would-be child escapologists, excursionists determined to disentangle themselves from their parents' branchlike arms. He re-fixed his tie and brushed his collar to oust any stray hair or abstract flakes of dandruff that had fallen like manna from heaven onto his single-breasted sand-coloured suit and examined the sunshine of his new shoes — all assertions of the importance of aesthetics and order in the presence of conformity and piety.

Giuseppe faintly recognized the scent of incense from the public rituals and parades he had witnessed as a child. He associated the scent with festivities and tasty street food. Back then, he would stand stock-still, a pagan spectator during the march of the observant, who trailed behind a blue-and-white statue carried by dignified-looking men from the neighbourhood. These men, in turn, followed in the footsteps of the same priest who had visited him the other day.

The interior of the church contained a Manichaean fragment of light and shadow, a corner of obscurity cut through by beams of light that passed directly through the grand window and illuminated the marble passageway on the floor. There were paintings everywhere, even high up on the ceiling, and images of half-naked men in Roman robes and flying angels, and several statues of Mary in various shapes and at various angles. Behind the altar was a large fresco of monks in long robes and sandals standing in a line, dwarfed by the figure of a distinguished man on horseback in military attire and dominating the image in stature, and clearly in importance.

Now — before the Babacci brothers had the chance to confront Giuseppe and call him a bastard again, or chant that malign melody in his ears, *What has your mother done . . . and now that the fox is gone . . . ?*, words he hadn't heard for years, not since his childhood — from afar emerged the same old priest whose frail little steps had climbed the stairs of his house the other day. The priest was walking towards him, then shaking his hand with enthusiasm and pride, and leading him to the front of the altar, all to the bewilderment and surprise of the congregation and Giuseppe himself.

For a long moment, he stood facing the crowd of familiar faces. But before the priest had a chance to speak, a roar arose from the rows of believers. They were looking at the Mussolini painting and looking back at Giuseppe, and a few of them even pointed at the artwork and then at him. A kid shouted, *C'est lui le monsieur sur le cheval, c'est il Duce!* — whereupon the priest turned to look at the portrait of Mussolini and then back at Giuseppe. He crossed himself. The hubbub of the congregation grew louder and louder, and as the organ began to play, Giuseppe stole a glance at the painting of the horse behind him and then at the man upon the horse.

He hurriedly left the church by the back alley that led to his apartment. Perhaps one of his mother's mysteries was in the process of explaining itself.

The next morning, Giuseppe handed over to the baker the letter that Sophia Loren had intended for his mother. The baker nodded and promised to drop by later.

That evening, Giuseppe opened the door to the baker, who had a shoebox under his arm. The baker put the box on the table, removed his apron, and washed his face and hands — just as he always used to do when he would sit down for supper with Giuseppe and his mother. But this time, after washing, he grabbed the box and went straight to Giuseppe's mother's bed. Giuseppe followed, and sat down beside him.

Your mother's correspondence, the baker said, and handed him the shoebox. She left it with me for fear that you might get the wrong idea.

Who are the letters from? Giuseppe asked.

It's correspondence with a lady in Italy, the baker said. Anna Maria Villani Scicolone, he added, with a sad flourish.

And who is she? Giuseppe asked again.

She is Sophia Loren's sister. And she's married to Mussolini's son, who is your half-brother.

Heat rushed to Giuseppe's face, as if the baker had just opened the oven door. He felt sad, not shocked but a deep sadness.

Your mother had an affair with Mussolini in her youth. She did it for a cause.

What cause? Giuseppe exclaimed.

The anti-fascist cause. The baker paused. She was from the same village as Mussolini. So, we secretly recruited her. We wanted her to get a job close to Mussolini himself, knowing he would trust her since she came from the same town. He liked people from his village. I think he even knew her father. By the time Mussolini found out that she was one of us, she was already pregnant.

With me?

Yes, with you, Giuseppe.

There was another brief moment of silence, and then the baker said, Mussolini wanted her dead. He wanted to assassinate her. We helped her escape the country. We smuggled her onto a boat, and then I decided to accompany her. We thought we'd end up in America. But the ship stopped in eastern

Canada, and since your mother spoke a little French that she'd learned from her grandmother, we thought we might break the journey in Montreal. I followed her wherever she went. I loved her. I always did. She never wanted to get married or live with me, or any man, except for you, her son. She was an independent woman. I never got married either. We stayed close and I got my job in the bakery and eventually became the owner, as you know. Your mother never wanted to get in touch with the Mussolini family until a few years ago. She never wanted you to know.

But she did contact them in the end?

Yes.

Why?

She'd tried to get in touch with Mussolini's son, your half-brother. She wrote to him, but he never replied. Then she sent a letter to his wife, Anna Maria, the sister of Sophia Loren, just to let the family know about your existence, and they corresponded for a while. Finally, your mother had to ask her for money. She had all kinds of proof that you were Il Duce's son. Your mother was sick by then, she knew she was dying. She was worried about you, the baker said. Worried that you'd have hardship without her. You had no one but her. Me? I am old and about to retire now, and your mother knew that my business goes badly, too.

So, Giuseppe said slowly, filling in the gaps, she asked Anna Maria for help. And the daughter-in-law of Mussolini sent her sister, the famous actress, to deliver the money.

Yes. Do you still need me to translate and read the letters to you? the baker said.

No, Giuseppe replied, after a pause.

Should I leave you the box?

No, said Giuseppe. You are the one who should keep it.

That night, Giuseppe walked to the church once more. He knocked at the priest's private door, and the cleric led him back to the altar.

Giuseppe studied the man on the horse, taking a long, close look at his father. He made his way around the altar and examined his father's eyes. He looked closely at every figure in the painting. Then he wept for a long time.

He left the church and returned home. There, he cast a long, pensive, melancholic look out the kitchen window at the alley lit by the same electric pole as always, at the same hackberry tree, at the old fence and the gravel road. And then he slowly packed his bag, made his mother's bed, took the rest of the money from the envelope and walked towards the train station. He caught a train to the port and waited until morning on a bench.

In the morning, he took a ship to Europe. For months, he was on the road with only the essentials: his camera, a few black-and-white films, a tripod that he carried on his shoulder like a defeated soldier with the front behind his back, and his packs of smokes. The rooms he stayed in along the way were often dirty and wretched, the people mean or aloof, and some smoked all night, and the fumes trespassed through the cardboard walls of his room, descending like a slow fog from bowed wooden ceilings.

In Paris, despite his meagre lodgings, he decided to stay awhile. But one day, while wandering aimlessly, he entered a museum and walked through galleries of portraits of people who looked dignified and powerful, the landscapes in their backgrounds colourful and pristine, and he imagined that the village of his mother — his parents — must be the same. Then and there, he decided to travel to the birthplace of the man on the horse.

Before he left Paris, he shot one roll of film and saved it in his bag. He would develop it one day, and it would be all that remained of him, a trace of his journey.

When Giuseppe finally reached the village of Predappio, he sat in the middle of the square, tired. A feeling of resentment combined with unexpected nostalgia came over him. The quiet was broken only by his own coughing. No more cigarettes, he told himself; he'd recently coughed up some blood.

He was almost out of money now, and so he walked around without plan or direction until he found himself in front of a souvenir store. On a whim, he stepped inside and found himself immediately surrounded by paraphernalia in his own image. Il Duce Souvenir Shop carried busts, calendars, ashtrays, beer glasses, key chains and black shirts with Roman eagles across the chest. The image of his father made him want to leave the store, but just as he turned to do so, the owner, a thickset man in a showy three-piece suit, appeared from behind the counter and said, *Prego*. Before Giuseppe could even nod in answer, the merchant froze, clearly struck by his customer's uncanny resemblance to the large Mussolini bust outside the store, and indeed to his entire shop's wares. His eyes wide, the shopkeeper crossed himself. Giuseppe tried to retreat, but the man stepped quickly forward and shook, then held, his hand, led him outside into the light, and carefully examined his face.

He asked Giuseppe his name.

Cassina, Giuseppe answered.

Cassina, the man repeated, twice, before grabbing his hand again and leading him a short walk down the street, to the gates of a cemetery. It was closed, but Giuseppe could see that the sign at its entry read "San Cassina."

Then the merchant brought him back to the store and offered him coffee and biscuits. He asked if Giuseppe had a place to stay, and Giuseppe explained that he'd used up almost all of his money travelling but had wanted to see his mother's village.

Soon, the merchant said, they will come. Soon, the pilgrims will come. Tomorrow, they will come to honour Il Duce's birthday.

Giuseppe devoured all he was offered: bread, cheese, ham, wine. The merchant watched him, insatiably curious: a Canadian, a carbon copy of Il Duce who spoke fluent Italian with a local accent, a total bewilderment.

Soon, the man said again, his voice contented, they will come.

Exhausted, Giuseppe stayed the night in the attic the merchant offered him above the store, but in the morning felt no better. He could hear a large crowd outside, disembarking from buses and gathering on the street. Blackshirts bearing flags took over the sidewalks. A parade was forming.

The merchant came up to the attic, a military uniform in hand, along with a fez, many decorations and ornaments, military shoes and a sword. He held the suit jacket against Giuseppe's shoulders and said, *Perfetto!* The same size as Il Duce! Try the outfit on, he urged.

Giuseppe refused. The man insisted. Giuseppe again refused, a cough shaking his body.

The merchant then detailed what Giuseppe owed him, counting up the food and drink and lodging. He threw the suit on the bed and waited outside the attic door, loudly recalculating food and accommodation expenses, including soap and water.

Eventually, Giuseppe emerged, dressed in the uniform, and the merchant started to weep and gesture and kiss the tips of his own prayer-joined fingers. He bustled around Giuseppe in a complex dance that alternated between reverence, submission, admiration and a sense of proprietorship.

Finally, he walked Giuseppe outside and stood him in front of the shop, and like a circus barker, he screamed, "IL DUCE! *Signore e Signori*, a photo for five lira, only five lira." Within minutes, a long line had formed, some spectators applauding, others chanting and waving flags, a few extending their arms in an upward salute. Still others were suspicious of the remarkable likeness before them. But for most, this living bust of Il Duce outside the store made the experience all the more miraculous. Soon, a crowd of hundreds formed around Giuseppe, who stifled his rattling cough as best he could while the merchant, sweaty in his shiny suit, started to sing, the group following his lead. The merchant skilfully positioned people next to Il Duce, held cameras, snapped pictures and collected payments. He even provided his own Polaroid and took instant photos for a higher price. Business was brisk, prosperous.

That evening, Giuseppe, still in his dictator attire, went up to the attic room and lay down, the sword by his side. He smoked between bouts of coughing, finished the bottle of wine on his bedside table, and looked over the photos of Paris he'd developed on the way to the village. On the reverse of one of them, he wrote a note to the great Italian actress Sophia Loren, scribbling his Predappio address at the end. He walked unsteadily to the post office and mailed the photo. On the way back, passing by the cemetery and his father's grave, he turned his head and spat.

At the shop, he asked the merchant for the money owed him for his day's work. The man paid him very little after deducting what was due for bed and board. Giuseppe tried to negotiate, but the merchant would not budge.

Waking in the damp attic room the next day, a pain lodged in his chest, Giuseppe felt too weak to get up. He covered himself and slept for most of the day, shivering and shuddering. Then he coughed through the night, and all through the following morning. As he fell into a hallucinatory state, he finally understood that the place his mother had so often described to him in her bedtime stories was the village called "Po." There, she would tell him, a monster was born. And the monster met a beautiful young girl, who loved a poor man . . . But often, then, his mother's stories would take a twist, and she would improvise tales of the lives of animals and various peripheral characters in a comic and tragic way. Giuseppe recalled a cunning fox and a bear that wore a hat with feathers and a horse that was always hungry — all of them phantoms in this mysterious, dangerous and fantastical place called Po that had remained with him all his life.

A day later, Giuseppe, the illegitimate son of the dictator, died. His body was found in bed, in the military attire that he had continued to wear for warmth.

He was buried in the village, not far from his father's monument. His headstone was humble, bearing the name Giuseppe Cassina and nothing else.

But a week later, a large black car with tinted windows arrived in the village and stopped across the road from the grave. The chauffeur hurried out to open the back door for a tall, elegant woman in dark glasses, wearing a large hat and carrying an expensive bag. She stepped out and walked over to the plain headstone and laid a bouquet of flowers against it. Then she turned and walked back to the vehicle; and moments later, like an apparition, she was whisked out of the cemetery and away.

INSTRUCTIONS FOR THE DANCE

IT WAS A GREY, rainy day in the fall of 1988 and the old walls of the city were damp and loveless, not suited for company or comfort. It was, however, a day fit for a brush with bureaucracy, and so Anatol Adamczyk walked over to the consulate in Warsaw, hoping the Communist Party had authorized his requested travel to Austria and would now provide him with the visa he needed. Inside, Anatol Adamczyk waited his turn on a metal chair, its cold iron surface inhospitable to his slender form. When his name was called, he proceeded to a counter where he sat facing a large opaque window. The voice of a woman floated out to him from behind the glass, sounding unusually cheerful for that of a state employee. Her tone was almost playful, and citizen Anatol was struck by the fact that none of his previous experiences of authority had contained this note of lightness and femininity.

The woman restated his name in a melodic, seemingly affectionate pitch and proceeded to ask him for his address and then the school he'd attended in his youth. The moment he mentioned that institution's name, the invisible woman behind the opaque glass released a lengthy hum of approval.

"So, you're *that* Anatol, the son of Jedrek and Helena Adamczyk?" she asked.

He nodded, then said yes aloud for fear that the melodic voice could not see him from behind the screen.

"Ah, then it was you who the dean kicked out of class in secondary school for singing that Krakowiak song and dancing while the teacher was gone?"

Anatol nodded and quietly chuckled at this sudden memory, and the voice behind the glass continued, "Our great nation proudly observes and deeply appreciates its significant folkloric tradition." Then the voice asked him in a whisper if he still owned the American denim jacket that he'd once worn to school every day. Anatol Adamczyk replied that he'd eventually had to sell that jacket because it did not fit him anymore. And then the lady behind the glass inquired if his mother still made her secret stroganoff, fragrant with cumin — the recipe that was kept hidden under the sink, concealed among the powders and detergents as if it were a precious gemstone that others might steal.

Now Anatol Adamczyk asked the glass a question: Did her mother still stand at the garden gate in her green apron and long rubber boots, a broom to chase shorty Bartek and the other boys away from the cherry tree in one hand, a cigarette in the other?

"Who could blame her for looking after such a beautiful tree?" queried the voice.

"My only regret," said Anatol flirtatiously, "is that I never got to taste the delicate fruit of that tree."

"In life, one should be ready to climb to the highest branch to get what one desires," the glass replied.

Then the voice asked in an official tone if he planned to finish film school when he returned from his trip.

Anatol Adamczyk remained silent.

A few minutes later, a page was slipped beneath the narrow opening in the glass, and he was free to leave the country. But before Anatol could lay the tips of his fingers on the paper, the lady's own fingers halted the document's retrieval. "I am meeting my mother at the station tonight at five," the voice said, swift and low. "She would love to offer you some sweet cherries to accompany you on your long journey."

Anatol found himself nodding wordlessly again, although he had no intention of accepting such dangerous fruit.

With the authorization signed, Anatol Adamczyk rushed home to pack only the essentials. He left behind all that was valuable and sentimental, took only his thin, light wallet and some clothing, and rushed to the station. He felt no need to check the train schedule. The glass had suggested a rendezvous at the station at five o'clock, and that was all he needed to know. If there was something you could count on in a totalitarian regime, it was the efficiency of prisons and trains.

Now, he told himself before entering the station, it is entirely possible that this is all a game. A teaser, where the glass will show up and arrest him. Or even worse, decide to leave with him. Which would certainly complicate everything. And how would she manage to grant herself an exit without the knowledge or consent of the state? One person leaving was enough of a risk; two would be seen as a serious defection. But then he thought: the glass could be his assurance that he'd be able to cross the border. Well, either way, he had no choice but to walk into whatever trap might be set. He shoved his documents into the inside pocket of his coat and walked into the building.

It was before five, and there was no sign of the glass. He imagined her wearing a red or burgundy dress, depending on the cherry season she'd had in mind. And a green hat, maybe, in place of a stem. He glanced anxiously around. A police officer passed nearby, and Anatol froze. Then the train arrived and still there was no sign of the glass. Maybe she was there among the few passengers on the platform, and although she would be able to spot him — she had seen him from behind her glass, after all — he was unable to recognize her?

Anatol boarded the train and waited. Soon he heard the whistle, and the locomotive's loud engine starting up . . . but still no glass. Perhaps she was already on the train. Bureaucrats do have their cruel and ludicrous ways of expressing love and laws in the same breath.

The train slowly left the city, passing industrial buildings stained with coal and heavy metals. And then came images of the landscape: a few trees, meadows rushing past the window. And no one showed up to greet him inside the train. The glass was certainly not on the train, Anatol decided, or she would have waited until this moment, when nature's beauty appeared, to slip in beside him with a smile. And so, to his bewilderment, no one came to join him. And when he crossed the border into Austria, he worried about her fate.

Anatol Adamczyk spent a year in Linz, and once he'd received his immigration papers, he left Austria for Winnipeg, Canada. Upon his arrival in that country, he started looking for work; but he had very little money and was quickly broke. Jobless, he stood on the street corner beside a grand hotel, laid his old hat on the ground, and started to sing and dance. He soon slipped on a patch of ice and sprained his wrist. The hotel doorman rushed over to help him, and through charm and good humour, Anatol quickly befriended the man and other staff who crowded round, and was soon hired as a bellboy, concealing his injury even though the pain was excruciating. He worked hard, using only his good arm, until, one day, catching his injured wrist on a door, he yelped in pain and was taken to hospital. There he met Ewa, a tall, beautiful woman also of Polish descent who worked part-time as a receptionist. She became his wife.

After the wedding, Anatol and Ewa decided to move to Montreal to live as two pseudo-French lovers, lost in a Nordic-style Francophonie, imitating film noir scenes, puffing smoke and playing sentimental French songs. Ewa began studying for a literature degree, and Anatol would make her laugh by pretending to be a baguette walking through the snow, slipping on the ice in dramatic style as he once had outside the hotel in Winnipeg. Their pursuit of an idyll — to spend their days in the manner of existentialists, drinking, smoking and engaging in ceaseless lovemaking — was challenging in their boxy little apartment, their lives financed only by small, occasional jobs. Her dream was to finish her degree and become a writer, and his was to return to film school and become a cinematographer.

In time, their dreams stalled. Eventually, Ewa landed a part-time job at a kindergarten, and Anatol began working as an assistant to a wedding photographer named Mike Gold, founder and sole owner of Gold Studios Inc.

Anatol's role was seasonal at first, and mostly involved weekends. But as Gold Studios Inc. grew, he was assigned more responsibilities, becoming the second photographer at the increasingly high-end studio. The clientele was wealthy, the weddings extravagant, sometimes even obscene in their untold expense and baroque settings. Anatol, with his photographic talent and his exuberant personality, excelled in his role. His connection to people was natural, playful and entertaining. His extravagant accent, his tall and genial presence, his combination of clownishness and courteous politesse extracted joy and laughter from every wedding party. He could appease dissatisfied mothers-in-law and make brides forget their aching ankles. He sang traditional tunes and even, on occasion, executed perfect pirouettes, camera in hand. He took off his shoes and stood on chairs, angling his camera down upon open smiles. In sumptuous hotel suites, he would hop from one piece of furniture to another, changing positions and perspectives. He toasted everyone, helped with the flowers, favourably appraised hairstyles, and took photos of the happy couple in bedrooms and bathrooms, on rooftops and balconies. At an Italian wedding, he was heard singing opera in the dressing room and seen flamboyantly kissing the hands of bridesmaids. At a Jewish wedding, he danced the hora from atop a chair in the centre of a circle of dancing Hasidim, their fingers intertwined, their hands in the air. In Vieux-Montréal, he took photos of a nervous groom and his striking best man barefoot in the fountain outside City Hall, and up in the Ferris wheel at the port. Once, Anatol was even spotted riding on the hood of a convertible, snapping newly-weds kissing in the back seat. He seemed to revolutionize the staid industry of wedding photography, and soon everyone asked after Anatol the dancer, Anatol bringer of joie de vivre. He was referenced at every wedding convention, became the recommendation of every priest, rabbi, hairdresser and florist, and was familiar to all the industry caterers, chauffeurs and tailors. He was known as the dancing photographer — although some thoughtlessly called him the Monkey for his camera antics, his shrill screams of "Smile!", his endless clicking, clicking. And soon the owner of the studio, Mike Gold, was less in demand than his assistant.

One Monday afternoon, Anatol the dancing photographer asked for a meeting with Mike Gold at the studio. He requested a stake in the business.

Mike Gold offered him a slight raise.

Anatol threatened to leave and start his own company.

Mike laughed and replied, "There's more to this business than dancing on tables and monkeying around."

Anatol borrowed money, maxed his credit cards and invested every penny he had in new equipment: two new cameras, a tripod, a camera bag and a bright flash. He also bought film. He contacted the many people he'd met at weddings and announced his new company name: Anatol Photography, Inc. He printed pamphlets. His business card featured his best black-and-white photograph, a bride and groom jumping in the air in the middle of a busy street. Freestyle, daring, fun images were his signature.

He went to hotels, churches and synagogues to promote his new company, but he had no office or studio space. He met clients at a coffee shop down the street from his apartment. The cheap-looking café, one of a chain, was depressing in appearance. Some clients were stunned by the presence of the poor and the unemployed, offended to be seated near tired and defeated old men in their cheap plaid jackets and synthetic baseball caps, nursing cold coffee and remorse, coughing into grubby tissues. The café's customers looked bitter, their hunger unsatisfied; theirs was a constant ancient thirst, their only fraternity solitude. The tables were stained, marked by spills and crumbs that Anatol brushed away with the back of his hand onto the slippery, greasy floor.

Worse, Anatol's own association with this joyless crowd alarmed his wealthy prospective clients. Anatol knew all the coffee drinkers by name, and even those who came to beg for change, confirming his clients' suspicion that he was himself a regular in this damp, lice-infested joint — a dancing photographer, perhaps, but not one they would care to commission.

Even the few demo portfolios that Anatol managed to put together were of cheap plastic, and the variety of packages he could offer was limited. The fees he quoted were too low or too high, not adequately calculated, even confusing, and with this confusion arose further suspicion and doubt. Now his accent seemed incomprehensibly thick, and his apparent unprofessionalism — the shoddy demos, the muddled pricing — made people wary and apprehensive about his capacity to deliver.

Anatol himself seemed changed: in his new venture, he felt obliged to conduct himself with an artificial formality when meeting new clients, a formality that was at odds with the idea he sold, that of the theatrical yet effective photography he was known for. And bereft of the tuxedo provided by Gold, he looked in perfect harmony with the drab and uninviting café. But the more he tried to change and improve things, the more he sank into debt. On Ewa's advice, he rented a temporary office to meet new clients, or on occasion hired a fancy car to visit them, but this did nothing but generate more debt and misery and yielded little work. He borrowed money from a loan shark. This is the only way forward, he told Ewa; one has to take chances in life, and I've come so far . . . The more he borrowed the more fearful Ewa became. The mood in the claustrophobic apartment turned bleak, the nights of playfully chasing each other around a distant memory, Anatol's impersonations of a lavishly accented French lover consigned to the past. All that was left were the bills spread over the desk like abandoned love letters.

The credit card people started calling the couple at home. They were late with the rent again, too, and Ewa's salary alone was not enough to keep the collection agencies and banks at bay. Anatol's pride prevented him from going back to Mike Gold, who now, in his mind, epitomized greed and evil. As his efforts to find work failed, his thoughts towards Gold turned to resentment and even violence, and he conjured up conspiracy theories and dark convictions about jealousy and sabotage.

One day, the loan shark's lackeys appeared at the café where Anatol sat with the poor. The muscle summoned him to a waiting car, where Mr. Shark was seated, making calls on his cellphone.

"You're late," was all Mr. Shark said.

Anatol tried to reassure the man by describing the revenue he expected from an upcoming wedding, by explaining the business trajectory he anticipated, and by blaming inclement weather and people's bad taste for his present predicament. His convoluted monologue alternated between wild assurances, rash promises and laying the blame for his debt on multiple third parties.

Mr. Shark, bored, had heard it all before. But then, suddenly, he raised his hand, and Anatol stopped, mid-sentence.

"You're in luck. My daughter is getting married in June and she needs a photographer." Mr. Shark handed Anatol a card with a phone number. "You arrange it with her. I'll see you at the wedding. Don't be late." He abruptly opened the door and let Anatol go.

Now Anatol was more confused than ever. Was the loan forgiven? Would he still have to pay? He chased after the car, which was stopped at nearby traffic lights. He knocked at the tinted window, and Mr. Shark lowered it halfway. Before Anatol had the chance to ask, the Shark said, "You still owe me, but I'll waive the interest and any payments until the day after the wedding."

Anatol stood in the middle of the street, cars honking as they passed him, a chill on his forehead, a cold sweat on his body. At that moment, he suddenly recalled the woman in Warsaw, the government official behind the opaque glass, his former schoolmate, Anna Dabrowski. It was his great misfortune, he thought, to be remembered. No one forgets me, he whispered to himself. My dancing is memorable. And somehow, everyone always finds me. What if he had met Anna at the station that rainy autumn day, as she had invited him to do? What if she had left with him for Linz, for Winnipeg, for Montreal? And what if he had never met Ewa? But, more puzzling to him now: Why had Anna taken so great a risk for him years ago, letting him leave the country when there was no reason to think he would ever return? Perhaps his dancing had saved him, he concluded. Anna had always been fond of his dancing at school, following him around as, mischievous and fun, he danced his way in and out of trouble, her face always laughing along. He recalled how one day he had danced with every other girl in the class but left her standing in the corner. He could picture her large, thick glasses and her bulky red shoes, poor Bartek alongside her. But perhaps, even so, she had understood that it was right for him to leave.

In the middle of the street, in despair at his plight, he started dancing through drivers' curses and blasting horns.

Anatol's father had been a dancer in a folkloric band, performing at official functions, dragging his son along to weddings and other formal events. He'd taught Anatol the art of dance, nurtured the performer within. Young Anatol would lift his head and put on a broad smile, and when his straight blond fringe fell into his eyes, he would flick it away with a winning toss of his head, his eye sparkling again. As the troupe of dancers stomped behind him, rocking the wooden platform, Anatol Adamczyk, the miracle kid, the beautiful boy, danced centre stage and got all the praise and attention.

Ewa received an inheritance from an aunt in Winnipeg. She cleared the credit card and bank debts without consulting Anatol, paid the back rent, kept the rest of the money herself and left him a letter on the kitchen table next to the overflowing ashtray, ending with the line, *I have paid your debts and I'll always love you, but this is the end*. Only the loan to Mr. Shark remained, but without Ewa, a seed of deep sadness lodged within Anatol. The symptoms of depression grew on his face, a deep-blue crescent under his eyes giving away his lack of slumber.

In those days of abandonment and poverty, his one consolation was the images he recalled of another place, *home*. He relived his childhood as a dancer, remembering his father's preparation for every event, meticulously unfolding the flashy, shiny suits, making sure his white-and-red outfit was immaculate. He thought of Anna too, the girl in his class who had fallen in love with his dancing steps and his charismatic energy; and he remembered intense, studious Bartek always seated at the desk behind hers. He ruminated over his visit to the consular office and Anna's invitation to meet at the station, and the date she had not kept.

After indulging in these memories for a time, Anatol rallied. He put his old hat on and went back out into the street, singing and dancing for food or money. The spare change he made wasn't enough to pay the rent, but the law said he could not be evicted in winter, he knew, and Ewa — through love or guilt, or perhaps sensing that he had borrowed even more than he had ever told her — sent a cheque in the mail that, if he lived very frugally, would not only cover the rent until the wedding but allow him to repay Mr. Shark in full. With no other money, and little food, he grew skinny, dancing in the cold and singing in the snow, moving only between the forlorn apartment, a soup kitchen and the welfare office. He tried not to get into fights with the other men in line. And he managed to survive on almost nothing until June.

On the day of the wedding, he took a long shower, shaved, put on his best suit — loose now on his thinner frame — and walked to the hotel to meet the bride at her suite. He looked older, sadder and broken, the joie de vivre that once had made his name dimmed. He was no longer as effortlessly charming, as natural and spontaneous as before; even to himself, his act seemed forced. But when he encountered five shrill, cheerful bridesmaids on his arrival at the hotel's opulent penthouse, he realized that the act was still within him, and that to be free of Mr. Shark, he would have to give himself over to the performance. He saw makeup artists splashing hues and fanning colours, hairdressers twisting locks with hot electric irons, boxes of corsages everywhere, dresses on hangers and food on large tables and flowers all around. When he accidentally entered the bedroom, he also saw the bride and two bridesmaids, half-naked, snorting cocaine off the dressing table, their noses pressed to a mirror.

The women greeted him and asked him not to take pictures of their lines but of their curves, and they ran their hands over their figures and laughed. He photographed them all; then the bride alone in her bra and underwear, holding her shoes against her face; then hugging and squeezing the other bridesmaids, jumping on the bed, blowing kisses at the camera. He used close-ups and wide-angled shots, documenting the nuptial preparations: the bride peeling a banana, the bride holding the banana next to her evocative lips, the bride kissing one of her bridesmaids, the bride now wearing a full white dress but showing off her stockings in the hallway, the bride running away with the bellhop down the corridor. This was his trademark style of liberated photography, a departure from the statue-stiff posing of the past — no drapes in the back of a studio, no elaborate lighting, no elongated divans, no fake Roman columns, but a hand-held, spontaneous-seeming encounter, pursuit, chase, reveal, a subversion or reversal of the old order, a dance before the wedding, marriage after sex, a new day, a new form of expression, everyone happy, free, a little rebellious.

When the bride's nose started to bleed and a minuscule droplet fell on her white dress, amid the panic and screaming, Anatol pulled out his old cotton handkerchief, calmly pressed it to the bride's nose, tilted her head back, pushed her gently onto a chair, gathered up the wrap of cocaine from the bedroom and carefully applied a little of the powder over the red dot on the front of the gown. He then proceeded with seltzer, dabbing the rest of the redness out, blow-drying the damp spot, and once the water had dried, he pulled the whitest pencil from the makeup kit and painted over the last faint shadow of blood. Then he resumed his camerawork.

At the wedding banquet, Anatol was received as if he was a guest, offered food, drink and drugs, even getting a pat on the back from a few of the Shark's menacing gorillas. When Mr. Shark himself approached and held the back of his neck and kissed his cheek, Anatol passed him an envelope of Ewa's banknotes. He had fulfilled his debt. Feeling free, he hopped on tables, took further photos, sang and even swung from a chandelier, the Monkey. He was asked to dance by one of the bridesmaids and woke up in bed the next morning beside her, both of them still fully clothed but crumpled, distorted and high.

After he delivered the photos to the bride's hotel the following night, he received a phone call from Mr. Shark. "All settled," the man said. "No one will bother you now."

The next morning, Anatol Adamczyk sold all his photography equipment and called Poland, asking for Anna Dabrowski at the government office in Warsaw. He was given numbers for several Annas, and he called them all, asking the distant voices on the line about a cherry tree. On one of the calls, after he'd posed his question, there was a long silence. Then the old saying: "In life, one should be ready to climb to the highest branch to get what one desires."

"If the branch still holds out desire to wanderers and strangers, then there's nothing that's out of reach."

He booked the first flight he could find heading homewards, a ticket to Berlin.

From there, he took a train east, past the fallen Wall, and, some hours beyond that, arrived at the central train station in Warsaw.

A woman with crazy hair, leopard-print pants and high heels, plastered in makeup and carrying a large handbag, walked towards him on the platform, smiling.

"Anatol, Anatol, what happened? What did those moose people do to you? It's me, Anna," the woman said. Anatol looked at her without speaking. "You don't recognize me after all these years." She laughed. "This way, let's go, my chauffeur is waiting. Welcome back to Poland."

Anatol followed, defeated, surprised, bewildered, exhausted.

The driver took his suitcase and opened the limousine door. He sat in the back, Anna beside him, still smiling. She opened the mini-bar and offered him a drink. As they drove, Anatol searched for markers of his youth out the window.

Eventually, they reached an area rich in luxury homes, gated gardens and expensive sports cars.

"Welcome to the Communist neighbourhood!" Anna cried, slapping him on the thigh, and both she and the chauffeur screamed with laughter.

The car drew up in front of a mansion. A maid was waiting at the door. Anatol was led to a guest room with a private bathroom. Later, he was summoned to dinner by a well-built young butler who ushered him into the dining room, vast as a banquet hall.

While Anna was in and out on business over the next few days, Anatol walked the streets of his old city feeling a deep melancholy. He was home, but he recognized little of it. His parents had died long before he'd left for Austria, and his childhood home had been lost, the area redeveloped. His sole link to this land seemed to be a woman he knew only from school who now moved in the world of the super-rich and resided behind wrought iron gates.

It was a grey, rainy day in the fall of 2004 when Anna knocked at Anatol's bedroom door, sat demurely on the edge of his bed and said, "You know, Anatol, I made good for myself. The old rulers become the new rulers, and what's new is only that we're much richer than they ever were. I have everything, as you can see. I have bodyguards, a chauffeur, other staff, a yoga instructor on call, and even a husband makes an appearance now and again. The only thing missing in my life is a dance teacher. You can stay as long as you like, but every evening when I'm home, I want a good glass of wine, music and someone to dance with. Not much to ask, is it?"

Anatol found himself nodding. "For how long?"

"Maybe a month, perhaps a lifetime, and I shall pay you handsomely," she said.

"Six months and then I should like to go," he tried bargaining. It was as if the opaque glass from that day long ago was between them once more.

"One dancing year, and then we can review things."

"We'll dance until the cherry season," he countered.

"Ah, you were always funny." She smiled.

The agreement made, the ritual commenced, and that night, the kitchen staff prepared dinner, drinks and music. After an interval, Anna and Anatol moved to the studio, where shoe tapping and laughing could be heard till the break of dawn.

The next evening, however, Anna did not appear. Nor the next night or the next.

A few days later, a large car with tinted windows pulled up in the driveway. Anna must be back, Anatol thought. Perhaps she'd been on a business trip at short notice.

None of the staff emerged to greet the car, so he took it upon himself to rush downstairs and open the door. A heavy giant of a man — Mr. Shark would have hired him on the spot — blocked the way entirely. He pushed Anatol back into the hall, followed him inside, looked around, went back out, nodded in the direction of the vehicle and opened the rear door.

A man the same age as Anatol, humbly dressed, emerged, beaming. He quickly fixed his jacket and approached Anatol with a broad smile — the biggest smile Anatol had encountered in days. Perhaps the man was not completely sober.

Oh, here you are, and as handsome as ever! Let's go inside, you're not going to leave me outside in the rain, are you, my old friend Anatol. Anatol, Anatol, don't you remember me, comrade?

Anatol looked intently at the man's face, then replied, "Yes, I do."

Who am I?

"Bartek," Anatol said.

Bartek released a very loud laugh. *Nice to see you, Anatol, Mr. Dance Instructor. I have always associated that job with homosexuals, but who knows what these Western countries can turn a man into? The goon stays outside, do not worry. He's just there to protect me from my many enemies. He doesn't see you as much of a threat. And if I were to be attacked by a dance instructor, it would only add to the misconception — among friends, let us call it a misconception — that I'm some kind of gangster. Anatol, Anatol, where are your manners? Bring us some drinks. Those Canadians made you lose your sense of hospitality.*

Anatol fetched a bottle of vodka and two glasses.

I see you are familiar with the bar in my house. Let's drink, comrade. To the return of the art of dancing in this country!

Anatol thought back to his school days. Bartek seemed impossibly unaltered after all these years, still as skinny and intense as he'd always been, his childlike voice unchanged. In his mind's eye, Anatol located Bartek's desk in their old classroom — always right behind Anna's, as a matter of fact. He'd been a shy, studious pupil and Anatol had never paid him much attention. Now Anatol wondered if he had ever joined the crowd in mocking Bartek, if he'd ever stolen his food or spat on his glasses.

Bartek sat on the carpet, glass in hand, and invited Anatol to sit beside him.

Anatol, Anatol, why did you leave us, why did you leave your country like a traitor?

Anatol said nothing.

Ah! You should have stayed. Those who leave never return the same, and the place they return to doesn't care about their "home-coming." You were always a romantic, a flamboyant romantic. The good-looking boy who all the girls in class chased after.

You are welcome to stay here until cherry season. A promise is a promise.

But Anatol, Anatol, you failed. You are a failure. You don't love your country. You only came back here because you had nowhere else to go. Ah, people's lives, Anatol, all of them so pathetic. Anatol, Anatol, you are probably wondering how your bookish fellow student Bartek, good, sensitive, literary Bartek, turned into a . . . well, among friends, let us say a big, powerful businessman.

Anatol, comrade, do you know the story about Aristotle — or, more likely, attributed to Aristotle — when he was accused of idleness because he had never worked, made money or meaningfully contributed to the wealth of society? He then made a point of making use of his empirical studies, his observations of nature's patterns, to predict the weather, and he planted crops accordingly. Soon he had a large yield, which made him immediately rich.

I confess, dear Anatol, that was me and not Aristotle. Every poem, every pearl of wisdom and every learned book I read in my youth, I used to move my way up the Party ranks. It is our treachery and greed that I have paid most attention to. Only two things drive a man to love power: greed and his own sense of the poetic.

You wouldn't understand. You probably don't read poetry now, and you were never much of a reader, you were always just a dancer. As our national poet Miłosz — remember him? — put it so eloquently:

> *We wanted to confess our sins but there were no takers.*
> *White clouds refused to accept them, and the wind*
> *Was too busy visiting sea after sea.*

The confessions I have to share, only a dancer would understand. To confess, my dear Anatol, is to elevate our whole body and being in its sorrows and joys.

And when one agrees to hear a confession, one has a duty to forgive.

Do you love Jesus, Anatol? For some people, a beautiful image is enough to make them offer love and be loyal. Once, Jesus was forbidden, but now we all love Jesus in this country — myself included. I love Jesus. Jesus forgives. Ah, my dear Anatol. Refill the glasses.

"And Anna?" Anatol asked, almost as a whisper.

Anna, of Anna you ask. Anna to whom I gave everything, Anna of whom I thought everything, she also confesses. And she has confessed to me her betrayal. And she only betrayed me when you came back, Anatol. She always loved you, only you.

The goon remains outside. I won't whistle for him to come and break your neck as long as you drink with me and listen to my confessions. Keep me company. I always loved Anna, and I followed her everywhere. The day she slipped you the exit paper to Linz, I was right there, I saw you through the glass. I was also there at the station to stop her. And I did stop her. I waited to see if she would go, and before she reached the station, I stopped her. I could have got rid of you, but she would never have forgiven me. Had she boarded a train with you, you would both have been detained and questioned.

Yes, I moved up the ranks faster than the speed of light. And you all thought that a lover of poetry, an avid reader, an intellectual like me would naturally be an opponent of the regime. The question is, why did I join the Party? Haven't you been dying to ask me?

"Well, to tell you the truth," Anatol said, confessing himself now, "I never thought about you much at all until today. But since you mention it, why did you join?"

I'll answer your question.

I signed up because, although I predicted the failure of Marxism, I still loved Marx's eloquence, yes, and his deep belief in an altruistic Christian world. That was sufficient to make me love the Party. I was always a believer in something. I was always seduced by the decadence of different religions and I had a deep affinity with the slavish morality that promotes triumph through false humility and nihilism. I belonged to that Party charade, and I worshipped Anna like I now love and worship Jesus.

And you, here you are, the very image of a shallow fly, always buzzing around, turning, mesmerizing every simple soul with your body's movements. The moment you left Poland I felt a relief. I could forget all about you. You were my last threat, you alone stood between me and Anna, even on the day you appeared behind the glass and I knew that you had come to beg for an exit. Indeed, it was me who authorized your visa. I knew you'd never make it elsewhere, but still, I never thought you'd be back. What are you, a dancing variety of homing pigeon? I should make you my latest sacrificial lamb ... but I have someone else in mind.

That day in the consulate when I let you leave, it was Miłosz again who came to my mind, his "Incantation":

Their friendship will be glorious, their time has no limit.
Their enemies have delivered themselves to destruction.

In reply and in anguish, Anatol cried out another verse from the same poem: "The news was brought to the mountains by a unicorn and an echo."

Bartek nodded in respect. *Ah, you do remember our poetry! You remember everything.*

Anatol, Anatol. Anna is no longer with us. Neither of us, not me, not you, will ever see her again. She's probably in transit now to somewhere quiet and very far away. Now let's dance together, just as slaughtered birds dance out their pain.

The old classmates drank, sang and danced for the rest of the night until the break of dawn. Then Bartek, summoning his guard, thanked Anatol for his loyalty and service, and recited another verse from the poet:

> *Short is your stay here:*
> *now and then at a matinal hour, if the sky is clear,*
> *in a melody repeated by a bird,*
> *or in the smell of apples at close of day*
> *when the light makes the orchards magic.*

Now, Bartek said. And he raised the guard's gun to his own temple and shot himself in the head.

The goon, as if he'd been expecting this, withdrew medical gloves from his side pocket and a body bag from behind the door, wrapped his master inside it and carried the remains to the car.

Anatol continued to stay in Anna's house, sleeping in the guest bedroom with its smart ensuite, drinking at the same table, eating dinner at the same time each day (though no one remained to make it for him). And every evening, he seemed to hear echoes of music and the sounds of dancers' feet flying across the empty studio floor.

Life continued this way until, one day, he saw from his window a burst of blossoms on a cherry tree. He opened the door and left the house. And that night, all the dancing, real and remembered, came to an end.

THE VEIL

When you find me, you shall never see me; when you lose me, you shall see me.

— Ibn 'Arabi, *Contemplation of the Holy Mysteries*

BAGHDAD, THAT ANCIENT CITY, was enduring in silence the unbearable warmth of the night. I went up to the roof of my house, looking for the breeze that had been promised me. I lay down on an old mattress that had known many generations of my family. Here, once, my grandfather had slept, and here my father had fallen asleep in his father's arms.

The city's heat poured out of my skin in a warm sweat, as if two mighty hands were squeezing my entrails in order to gather their liquid before running off to drink, share, wave and dance at a virgin's wedding. I looked up at the sky and saw a vast emptiness. At this hour, in one motion, the breath of all mothers, like a swift stroke from an omnipotent sword, puffed out from behind pursed lips and sent the flames of a million candles into death and darkness. The city was dimmed; tiny lights bowed and retired. And suddenly, oh! Your mighty light was revealed to me, as if seventy thousand black veils had been dropped to cover the city and expose the fourteen stars that bestowed wonder and knowledge. Now my eyes shall embrace you, and watch you in your unattainable dwelling, and seek to join your light.

A loud knock on the door below me — and the sound brought me back from my journey, making me lose your path. I stood up, ran down the stairs, crossed the living room and pulled open the old wooden door. There stood two large men, their faces hidden in the quiet night.

"Are you Professor Idris?" asked a voice.

"Yes, I am. Who is asking?" I replied.

"The Ministry of Justice and Peace."

I looked for a candle, found one; looked for a match, lit it. I invited the men to enter and offered them seats. My wife, Zahra, woke up, and I asked her to make coffee. Who are these men? she asked me. What do they want?

I do not know. Make the coffee.

Did anyone die? What did you do? What hour is it? Where were you? Her face twitched as her hands searched the kitchen counter looking for spoons, water, the coffee pot.

I went back to my guests and sat down with them. The feeble, dancing flame of a short candle revealed their serious faces. Fate laughed and stood outside the door, waiting.

"You understand, read and write English, Professor Idris?" one man asked.

"Yes," I said.

"You studied law in England."

"Yes."

"And you were drafted and sent to Mosul in the Iran–Iraq War."

"Yes."

"Taught at the university in Baghdad. Married to Zahra al-Aoumih."

"Yes."

"Had a child who died young, during the American embargo on our people."

"Yes, that is me," I said.

"Could you please come with us, Professor?"

As we stood up, my wife appeared with two cups in her hands and fear on her face. She greeted the men with utter stillness. She asked me where I was going, avoiding any direct questioning of our guests. I looked at the man in charge, hoping he would answer, but he ignored the woman, my wife, and walked towards the door.

I got dressed in my regular clothes. My wife was in tears, asking when I would be back, how long I would be away. She walked back and forth, at times coming towards me, at other times towards the officials, holding out her hands, touching my shoulders, whispering, asking me the same questions again and again.

I left the house and faced the night. I climbed into the waiting military car. When I looked back, I saw Zahra standing at the door, covered in grief — long, empty, wretched nights slowly creeping up beside her.

The man drove the car like a soldier eager to return home. On our way, a warm khamsin wind passed me by, brushing my face in a violent rush and making me weep. As the moon watched, we drove past plains, long, dusty roads and empty meadows waiting for dawn and salvation.

Eventually, I slept. When at last we stopped, I woke up, got out and walked away from the car, following the men in the grey suits. We entered a building with empty, dirty hallways flooded with the smells of urine and dampness. We descended long, narrow stairs. I heard metal doors closing, booming, sending me omens of large spaces and faraway structures. I was led to a room with green, faded walls, a dusty metal desk, a pale light, a chair and a framed photograph of a man, a ruler, hung high beyond my reach. I was left alone with the sound of my own heavy breathing, repeated and brought back to me as a weak, confined echo.

I waited. I paced. I thought of Zahra standing at the old door to my home. I began to think about the reason for my being there. Was it something I had said? Something I had written? Something I had whispered to a friend? Was it that night in battle when I had spared the life of a soldier? Should I have shot him? How could I have? He was almost the age of my son. My son! Now Zahra was alone. My son was dead. I was here, tired. I was eager to know why. I am innocent, I reassured myself. I have nothing to fear. I can defend myself, no matter what the accusation. The men who brought me here were respectful, though. They knew all about me. My history! They knew my history. English! Why did they ask about my fluency in English? England. Yes! That is it. I am a suspect. England, yes. It is something to do with that old empire. But I was young, and it was a long time ago. What did I do then? Why now? . . .

Suddenly, the dim light that hung from the ceiling went out, and I was left in darkness. I extended my arms, moving cautiously and with confusion. I felt moist walls. Then, as if there were a demon in my chest, I ran around frantically in all directions. Finally, I held on to the chair, edged around it and sat on the seat. I tried to remember my position, to locate myself. Where had the objects around me been placed? Yes! The leader's image was behind and above me, the desk was on my left, the door . . . Yes! The door was on the other side. Now I felt more stable, less distressed. I decided to stay in my chair. I shouted, Darkness! My enemy! Oh, how I long for a glance of your unattainable light, my light. Silence! Blindness! I am a pearl in an abyss. I am a wild bird trapped in an attic.

I am an unburied corpse left on the surface for vultures to tear up and fight over. I am in hell!

I began to panic, but then made a conscious effort to stop. My eyes will adjust, and I will see shapes again, I reassured myself. But soon I realized I must be under the ground. I shivered. I started to rock in my chair and hum. I tried to guess what hour it was and became obsessed with the time. I decided to recall and retrace the events of the day, trying not to think of Zahra. I figured the men had reached my house at eleven in the evening, and it had taken us two hours on the road to reach this place. But how long had I been here? . . . I had lost track. In an attempt to stop the madness, I decided to settle on an hour. It is three in the morning, I proclaimed to myself, and that is that. My eyelids were heavy, but for a long time, I tried to resist falling asleep. A mixture of anticipation and fear helped me. But then, *Tired, now you are tired*, I finally told myself. I slept and waited for your dreams to come.

The next morning, I was led to a room with a window and a view. Here I waited. After a little while, an official in a suit appeared and shook my hand. He offered me coffee, a cigarette, and brought me something to eat.

"Eat and get some strength, and we will talk later, Professor," he said.

I devoured what was given to me. I smoked the cigarette.

I drank water and stared at a beam of light that had landed on the floor. I rejoiced at seeing the light, and I smiled and hailed your presence.

The official handed me another cigarette. I thanked him and declined, but then I changed my mind, took it and kept it, unlit, juggling it between my fingers.

The man had a thick, calm voice. He inhaled the smoke of his own cigarette and released it out of his nostrils. He sat at the desk and shuffled some papers. Then he started to read. At times, he would glance at me with a blank expression; other times, he would nod and acknowledge my presence.

"Professor Idris," he said to me all of a sudden, making my heart beat and my blood rush. *Verdict!* I shouted within my own mind. *Yes! Finally. Talk to me, your holiness, you grand orator. Release me from your claws. Utter. Words. In the beginning, there was the Word. I am all ears.* A foam of rage and anticipation filled my mouth, a white liquid full of hidden venom I was waiting to spit. *Talk, my Lord. Proclaim and retreat. Your humble servant is not worthy of your dungeon; my hands are too thin for your chains. SPEAK!*

And the official said: "You are a good, respectful man, Professor Idris. We have nothing against you. I should clarify the reason for your presence here. In simple terms, we brought you here because of your integrity, Professor, and your loyalty to this great country of ours . . . and because we need your assistance in a top secret affair."

He gave me a speech full of praise and patriotic rhetoric. I had a mission to fulfill, he said. He talked about a secret American delegation that was in our country for talk and negotiations. My mission, he said, was to assist in the translation of important documents. "It is a simple matter for a well-educated man like you, Professor. Nevertheless, the task is important to this great nation of ours," he said.

I nodded. For a moment, I felt like reciprocating his words with a speech on my loyalty and eagerness to serve, but I stopped, fearing that my tired body and weary spirit would reveal my indifference to it all. I felt resentment over being brought to this place against my will. But I willed my resentment to stay hidden. I feared that a refusal to co-operate might lead to my death. And my death might keep me from reaching your light.

"Professor, are you willing to help your country?" the official asked me suddenly, looking me straight in the eyes.

"Yes." I bowed my head in a fake, treacherous act of submission and devotion. "I will do everything to help this great nation of ours," I added with the voice of a soldier, the love of a woman and the prayer of an old, pious man.

"Correct," the man said. "Correct." And he nodded. "Professor, come with me. I shall introduce you to the Americans."

He, the smoker, the calm inquisitor, the man who held me, opened the door and bowed his head in a gesture meant to guide me in a straight, forward line and lead me through the frame of steel. I crossed the room's boundary and stepped out into the hallway, where I was met by an unshaven soldier in a green combat suit, a machine gun draped across his belly.

I walked behind the official; the soldier followed us both. We went up some stairs and through another hallway and up more stairs. I walked slowly, trailing behind the official, and the soldier placed his hand on my left shoulder and pushed me forward. I looked back and saw his piercing eyes, his red face, his hand on the trigger of his gun, his cold blood, his yellow teeth — and I felt anger at his touch. I ran up closer to the official and tried to walk by his side. The soldier quickened his pace. Then I slowed down suddenly, which made my guardian lose his step and bump into me. I started to enjoy our little game and decided to take it a little further. I turned into the wrong hallway and acted like I was lost and confused. The soldier ran in a panic after me, gripping my shoulder, his fingernails almost penetrating my skin as he pushed me back towards the official.

At last, we arrived at our destination, and the official asked me to wait at the door. I was alone with the fighter. He stayed glued to me, alert. I asked him for a cigarette. He just looked at me and kept silent. I began to babble about the beauty of the place we were in, and how I had enjoyed a good sound sleep in the quiet, perfumed room that had been assigned to me last night. I asked him what time they delivered breakfast in the morning and if the car would come soon to take me back to my wife. I asked him if I could have some books to read and music to listen to, preferably Nazim al-Ghazali. Then I asked him if he had a wife and children. He looked straight at me and shook his head in disbelief.

The official came out of the room on tiptoe. Holding the doorknob carefully, he gently closed the door behind him and spoke to me in a low voice. "Professor Idris, there is a meeting in here between our commanders and the American delegation. Professor, you are to assist in the translation of documents when needed. Is that clear?"

"All clear," I said, and restrained a reflex to salute.

The official went back in; a few minutes later, he called for me. I stepped into the room slowly, stretching my head forward, measuring and weighing my steps carefully. The official grasped me by the sleeve and pulled me farther into the room — right into the middle of it. "The translator is here," he said in an unexpectedly loud voice. "This is Professor Idris." Then he took a step back.

The room had a large table stretching from one end to the other and dividing the space into two parallel segments: floor to table, table to ceiling. Between the two spaces, there was an Iraqi colonel and a few subordinates on one side and, on the other, a woman leaning over a map, casting a shadow on rivers, plains and mountains. There was a man in a civilian suit next to the woman. She looked my way, arranged her skirt, moved forward and stretched out her hand.

"I am Mrs. Yalda," she said, "and this is Bob." She pointed at the man next to her.

We shook hands. Mrs. Yalda looked me straight in the eye, pressing my hand with a firm handshake. Then, suddenly, she pulled her hand away. I smiled timidly and started to apologize for my sweaty, dirty hands — hands that had infected hers with traces of fluid. I stuttered and mumbled in English like an old servant who had just dropped the afternoon tea on a lady's lap. She ignored me and went back to looking at the map, rubbing her hands clean.

Mrs. Yalda had a tiny, pointed nose, sunken eyes, thin eyelashes and clear white skin. She was short with wide, bulky shoulders. She was in her late fifties or early sixties. Her formal and polite manner clearly stated the importance of her position. She held a poor, lonely pencil like a whip between her fingers, tapping it on her thin lips from time to time.

On the other side of the table sat the colonel, rigid. Two insignificant soldiers stood firmly behind him at a short distance, giving the three of them the triangular shape that, I had noticed over the years, military men like to assume on official occasions.

I sat on a chair in a corner and waited. I watched the two sides preparing for their duel. The colonel was calm, observing his opponent with an air of indifference. Mrs. Yalda retrieved her glasses and opened up the arms. She placed them on her face. Now she saw letters, words and polished numbers. She started reading out a list in concise phrases:

Exploration and production contract
Building local expertise
Oil revenue
Regulation of petroleum operation
Access to zones subject to maritime jurisdiction
Inspection
Et cetera.

At this, the colonel smiled, shook his head, lifted his cup of coffee and drank. He lit his cigarette, inhaled, exhaled and looked at the woman. Then, in Arabic that was translated by one of the soldiers standing behind him, he said, "I am here today on behalf of our commander to welcome you to our proud nation. Our custom is to greet guests and enemies alike before conducting any business. As you have seen, we have a translator and a professor in international law here with us today, who, in complete secrecy, will translate any document you have for us."

A thin, sarcastic smile appeared below his thick moustache.

Mrs. Yalda sank backwards in her chair and threw the pencil on the table. It bounced off the pile of paper and rolled sideways onto the wooden surface of the table. "Well then, we'll resume when the translation is ready. Thank your commander for me and do tell him that I am a busy woman and have no time to spare," she said. She stood up.

Bob picked up the papers from left to right. Mrs. Yalda fixed her suit and headed to the door. The colonel stayed where he was, puffing smoke in the air.

I was led back to my room by the same soldier who had escorted me earlier. The official accompanied us and asked me if I was capable of doing the job. Without waiting for my answer, he explained what was to come. How long will I be here? I asked. *It all depends*, he said. I asked him if I might have a better room to stay in, with a bed, and some food. He nodded; all this would be arranged. He apologized for the accommodations of the previous night, explaining that they'd had to find a translator in a hurry, that they couldn't trust just anyone with the job, that for security reasons it had to be someone from outside government circles. He reminded me of the secrecy of the operation and praised my patience, my loyalty and my sacrifice to this land.

I mumbled something incomprehensible to men and gods alike, thinking of the promised food and water. But to my despair, I was led back to the room in the basement. A sense of melancholy washed over me and left me stranded on the one chair, motionless. Now there will be emptiness again, I thought. Tonight, ghosts of misery will invite themselves in and feast upon my sorrow, leaving me in hunger and solitude.

Wretched is my land, I thought. The devil, dressed in a woman's gown, is here to claim victory and I am to witness it all. Tyrants within, and vultures above. *Lamentation is our history*, my father always said.

The door opened and I was led to another room with a bed and a table. That door slammed behind me, and I heard the keys of my jailer clink, filling the emptiness and turning my liberty upside down.

Now, even the moon was leaving. Through a small window above my head, I watched it fading into absence. Darkness was here again. Or maybe darkness had never left.

I lay on the metal bed. A thick old cover, made of wool and stained by prisoners' tears, had been left on the mattress. It was full of wrinkles and body smells.

My eyes closed. I slept.

Early the next morning, dawn shivered and awoke. A beam of bold light made its way through the window above, touched part of the wall and shone into the room with all its might. Now all was revealed: the walls were covered with letters, drawings, poems, epics. There were words drawn by jailed men's fingers, Qur'anic verses uttered by the pious, calendars memorized by the impatient, prayers recited by the redeemed and a woman's face enshrined by the talented. It was morning, and morning is your wife's body naked and warm under white sheets and over all norms and taboos; morning is your son jumping on your belly and asking you to play. Morning is Arabic coffee thrown into boiling water, then lifted and thrown back by a delicate hand. Morning is bread dipped in curved brown plates. Morning is when the bombs stop. Morning is the death of a son. All mornings are that one morning when we rushed to the hospital, my child in his mother's arms. Morning is the long line and empty shelves, helpless doctors and wailing women. Morning is disease and death, poverty and black veils. Morning is a small coffin and loud chants. Morning is when I went back to you, after my son's death. Morning is when I prayed to you and returned to your holy realm.

Around noon, I was fed, and later in the afternoon, I was called back to the conference room. Bob was waiting for me. He handed me a piece of paper and asked me to translate it into Arabic. I read: "WHEREAS the rehabilitation and further development of industry will be enhanced by the participation of international and national investors of recognized technical, managerial and operational skills as well as robust resources . . ."

Through the bars of the open window, I heard cars in the street halting suddenly, and doors slamming. I saw dust flying into the air. Convoys of soldiers and diplomats entered

the building in a rush, and soon found their way to the
room. The colonel, Mrs. Yalda and many other officials
took their seats.

Documents were laid down. Positions were assumed.
Defiant glances were exchanged.

Hours and days of negotiations passed. I stood there,
translating, explaining, writing. I worked long hours. I ate
with the soldiers. I never left the building. I longed to see my
wife, my home, my land and its demolished streets, its worn-
out people.

In the evenings, feeble sounds escaped from the night
guard's radio and carried songs along the hallway and into
my cell, sweet tunes like little steps that danced, reminding
me of different times.

Once, in the cell, I danced. Once, within its walls, I slept.
The rest of the time, I worked, prayed and dreamed.

More days passed. My room had a desk now, the food had
improved, and the guards called me by name. But the toilets
down the hallway were filthy, the water scarce, and the routine
left me in a state of boredom and anger.

I dealt with Bob daily; his quiet, polite manners irritated
me. His objections and explanations were always presented in
an indirect, subtle, slow manner, which I thought was a waste
of time. Every other day, I would meet with Mrs. Yalda.

In one of these sessions, she asked Bob to go fetch a document. The technocrat ran out of the room, an obedient servant.

Mrs. Yalda held up a paper and moved closer to me. "Are you married, Professor?" she asked.

"Yes."

"One wife?"

I ignored her and looked at the paper.

"Kids?"

"One who died."

"Sorry," she said.

"No, you are not," I said in a sudden burst. "Mrs. Yalda" — I called her by her name for the first time — "it is your policies, it is your embargo, that killed my child."

"Do not blame us, Professor. Blame the government that was oppressing you all," she said.

"I am not blaming, I am accusing," I said, and felt a violent rush of desire for revenge. I wanted blood, or a knife, or poison.

"Professor, what do you think will happen to you after these meetings are over? Do you think they will let you go back to your wife? I worry about you, Mr. Idris. I was talking to Bob the other day. We both worry about your fate. You have been exposed to a substantial amount of classified information. I hope your government trusts you, I do hope so."

I kept silent. I thought of my wife.

"There is not much water in this place, Professor. Do they let you shower? Don't feel embarrassed," she said. "I like how the Middle East smells. The natural smell, you know. I love the food, too. I have always loved the food."

I reached for a file and moved away.

When Bob returned, I called for the guard — whose name, I knew now, was Hassan — and left.

That night, I felt dizzy. Fever, heatstroke, thirst, weakness came over me. I became delirious. I was in pain and nauseated. I shouted to the guard in vain. "Hassan!" I shouted. "Bring me water, Hassan!" My shouts were feeble. They must have sounded like a series of mumbles. But I know you heard me.

In my delirium, I repeated your name a thousand times. Finally, I slept, and I waited for you in my dreams. I had a vision of your light. I heard your call. I prayed again.

I was sick for the next few days. The official promised to bring a military doctor, but I waited in vain for that doctor to show up.

Hassan, the guard, kept saying to me, "Praise Allah and have faith, Professor."

"Faith," I said. "Faith is all that is left to us."

Hassan sat on the chair beside my bed and whispered, "Professor, I've read everything, and I know."

"What do you know?"

"I know that they are here to take everything from us."

"Then you are more than a guard, Hassan."

"Listen to me well," Hassan said. "The colonel should not sign those papers. If you are a believer, you should stop this."

"What are you talking about? Who are you?"

"I am the one who fears only God," he said. "Listen, Professor, listen well. Your only salvation is with me."

"I have a fever," I said.

"Listen. After you're done with this, I am ordered to kill you and your wife."

I felt nauseous and weak. "Who? Why . . . ? Zahra . . ." I mumbled.

"Professor, there is only one thing to do. This should be stopped. There is only one way out of this."

The next morning, in spite of my fragile state, I was led upstairs to Mrs. Yalda. Hassan held my arm and guided me slowly through the corridors and up the stairs. When I reached the conference room, I greeted the lady and offered her my feeble bones, my sweat and my hidden hate for what she represented to me now.

"My son," I mumbled to her.

"This man is dying," Mrs. Yalda said in a loud, protesting voice.

I felt a sour liquid bursting out of my stomach in a rush and filling my mouth. I tried to repress it, but my lips failed me. I ran to the corner and vomited. Lumps of yellow water splashed onto the cement floor like the explosions of a surgical-strike bomb dropped from a high plane above.

I vomited Mrs. Yalda, I vomited hamburger-chain restaurants, Hollywood game shows, fat farmers full of hormone-laced cows, long highways, corporate suits, silk ties and chained dogs, white houses, green lawns, feather pillows and tiger skins, sticks and badges, bags and shoppers, dealers and weapons, microphones and elected voices. My vomit was endless.

Hassan came over and offered me a dirty cloth to wipe my mouth. Then he took hold of my arm, tugged on it meaningfully and whispered, "Grab it!" I grabbed Hassan's gun and pushed him back. I aimed the firearm at Mrs. Yalda. I fired. I fired until all nine rounds were empty. Mrs. Yalda's body fell; blood stained her white shirt.

Hassan jumped at me, took back his gun and twisted my arm. He held me by the neck and pressed my face on the table. I heard soldiers' feet running in panic through hallways. I heard shouts and confusion. But I stayed calm. I watched Bob crawl into a corner, his hands on his head, moaning like a dog. I saw his eyeglasses, fallen on the floor.

For the next few days, I was beaten by Hassan and many other men, interrogated and called a spy.

I was cuffed and left in a tiny cell. A thick black cloth was secured over my eyes.

I thought of Zahra. I thought of my son, and then I thought of my existence. I passed the days that followed in fasting and prayer. No veil shall obstruct your light. I repeated this chant until the veil dropped and you were revealed to me.

Now I have found you, but I cannot see you.

Now I am standing, facing your light, but I have lost you. Only nothingness knows existence. And I repeated his words: whoever loses me, finds me; and whoever finds me no longer loses me. When you find me, you shall never see me; when you lose me, you shall see me.

Now I see again your reflection, in the swift stroke from an omnipotent sword coming towards me. Now I see the moon gathering up all its scattered light. You threw veils over it to complete its absence. Only nothingness knows existence.

THE DUPLICATES

BASILIDIS AL AWAD WORKED in the library at McGill University, in the department of archives. He was a meticulous man, an autodidact, erudite and eloquent and, as you might expect, technically adept in the delicate process of photographic reproduction of valuable manuscripts. He was a master of analog photography and in private would often theorize on the role theology and the Enlightenment had played in the evolution of the medium. Al Awad believed that humans' obsession with the passage of time, our insistence that existence must mean something, was merely an attempt to preserve an image of our fleeting reality.

As for the technical side of his profession, lighting, measurements and the precision of photographic mechanisms were all challenges that Al Awad was eager to solve. This split in his character — between Al Awad the theologian and Al Awad the mechanical engineer — had caused him to hesitate between two career paths. It took years for him to discover in photography the common thread that connected his areas of interest.

He was an odd man, a loner who preferred the company of books and the faint perfume of cellulose nitrate on mouldy old papers to the sweet smell of a woman. His considerable intellect suggested that he could have held a significant post in government or a prestigious academic position, but he was held back by his inadequacies in public, his poor social skills and extreme shyness. His laconic sentences were often mumbled and emerged in a fashion that was either choleric or chaotic, but his work was always efficient and exact, making him seem irreplaceable. His presence was eerie, with his great height elongated by his upright posture, his long hair anointed with oil, the daunting thickness of his eyeglasses, and he endeared himself to only a select few librarians who thought they understood the source of his oddness and sympathized with his need for seclusion. He was capable of duplicating absolutely anything, though he himself was unique.

The collection in the library's archive that Al Awad most prized contained nineteenth-century glass-plate negatives. He never missed an opportunity to hold and examine the fragile glass spotted with disbursed poisonous chemicals, the hand-coloured plates faded with time, occasionally cracked. *My precious little vitrines,* he called them with affection. Some depicted the West during the Victorian era, but to him, the most precious were the old orientalist plates depicting Moroccan prostitutes, or Anglo-American travellers posing in front of the pyramids and other monuments, or high-society ladies with large hats and parasols blocking the sizzling Eastern sun, or a series from his ancestral land, portraits taken by the Jesuits of the Maronite community in the high mountains of the Levant.

Al Awad had many philosophical reservations and observations about aspects of photography and often disagreed with how the medium was presented in the books and theses he read avidly, but he was incapable of writing a word on these topics to refute the arguments himself. Such was his fate — the fate of a reader thoroughly steeped in the detail of the medium but inexperienced in both academia and its artful methodologies. When Walter Benjamin, in his famous essay "The Work of Art in the Age of Mechanical Reproduction," wrote about the democratization of art through photography, and the loss of aura and uniqueness in reproducible art objects, Basilidis Al Awad would object to himself: But why do we assume that the aura of a unique work is not retained in the negative or by the final photographic image? For Al Awad, that secret plate, the negative, was wrongly overlooked as an art object in itself, always considered a mere part of production, a step towards the end result, when really it possessed an aura entirely its own, separate from the processes of reproduction. In Al Awad's passionate argument to himself, Benjamin was subconsciously applying a political and technical hierarchy, and also making a deficient comparison between the photographic negative and the theological concept of the seen and unseen. The essential technical elements required for any reproduction were being excluded on political grounds from possessing the rightful aesthetic aura of the image, the photograph. Yet in Al Awad's view, those glass plates, and even the more modern strips of plastic negatives, were as unique as any original painting. Furthermore, he rejected the word *negative* itself. It implied a devaluation. Clearly, Benjamin had fallen into the capitalist trap of being distracted by the final product and its process of distribution, and not the obscure source, the zone where the reproduction process itself constitutes the aura of the object. *Nothing about you is lesser*, he would say to the glass plates as he slowly, gently laid them in their archival boxes.

Negatives for Al Awad were never simply a utilitarian tool; he did not distinguish between the functional and the poetic in them. Rather, he considered that all photographs or "positives" possessed multiple personalities, split identities, reproduced as they were in the hundreds or even the millions, while *only* the negative retained its singular authenticity. But when does a photograph begin and end? he asked himself. Then he would answer himself: When did God begin and end? The chain of production was not cyclical but linear. It started with the past existence of a photographed object that transformed into another object that itself would eventually deteriorate or lose its meaning. As the world outside passed through its seasons, Al Awad spent his time reflecting on such hallucinatory questions of appearance and disappearance.

Sometimes, inside his darkroom, Al Awad would pause, fearing to print the "positives" that would reveal the images held on the negative glass. Perhaps the faces in the glass should remain unknown, he would opine, following the old iconoclastic doctrines. The dark zones on glass-plate negatives, viewed at a certain angle, reflected the silver-blue hue of mercury. That dark veneer, if printed, would reveal areas of bright sunlight on the paper copy, and the light zones on the negative would then introduce shadow and darkness onto the image. "Yet now, with selfish pride and most impious madness, and at the risk of being punished in everlasting darkness," Al Awad would murmur to himself, citing the *Confessions* of Saint Augustine, that Manichaean dualist, that deserter, that African forger of faith, "they perversely oppose that name under which they fraudulently protected themselves for the sake of enjoying the light of this brief life."

Occasionally, Basilidis Al Awad would be given a particularly delicate assignment, photographing a rare and valuable manuscript. On those days, he would position the document on the copy table, angle his large camera right above the paper, perpendicularly, like the midday sun, or as if taking a bird's-eye view of terrain below. Two lights would be positioned on either side of the book, facing one another at a forty-five-degree angle, and he would proceed to click and copy. He would read the contents of the manuscript as he worked, storing everything in his photographic memory, and would later remember by heart the selected page or fragment he had copied — even the catalogue or lecture for which it had been prepared. Few languages were an obstacle — he had a command of ancient ones, and his preference was for the Semitic languages, Aramaic, Hebrew, Arabic and Phoenician.

Before every delicate operation — which was how Al Awad thought of this work — he would re-comb his oiled hair to keep it out of harm's way, refrain from shaking hands or touching handrails or elevator buttons, and use cutlery during his meals with fastidious care in order not to contaminate in any way the valuable manuscripts. It was only when pulling on library-issue white cotton gloves before the job that he felt a rare instance of self-consciousness. Why do these gloves have to be white? he would wonder. He never minded the feel of the cotton between his large fingers, but the colour always concerned him: he was afraid that the reflective white would bounce light off his hands and affect the exposure.

One particular day, Al Awad was photographing a manuscript on loan to the library from the Vatican. He was ecstatic at the prospect. This manuscript alone, among all the duplicates he had previously made, touched him personally.

It was a text drafted by Giuseppe Simone Assemani (whose many names in other languages he knew well — in Arabic, يوسف بن سمعان السمعاني or Yusuf ibn Siman as-Simani; in English, Joseph Simon Assemani; in Latin, Joseph Simonius Assemanus), to whom Al Awad claimed a connection as one of his descendants. The scripture was to be displayed as part of an exhibit on Near East codices. It was an early manuscript of *The Hymns on Virginity* by Ephrem the Syrian, with a note and Latin translations in the margins by Assemani himself.

Once Al Awad had possession of the text, he sat in his favourite corner, next to a special lamp. Wearing his white gloves, he laid the folder on the table and looked at it. It was a series of songs, a glorification of God, prayers written in the Syriac dialect of Aramaic, words whose melodic incantations had later found their way into Qur'anic texts — at least, this was Al Awad's opinion, although he had never dared articulate it aloud. He regarded the work of Ephrem the Syrian as poetry worthy of comparison with the Psalms, similarly adulatory yet orthodox. That Syrian priest had been a hard-liner, Al Awad believed, a virtuoso poet of orthodoxy. The Latin translation in his forebear's own hand made Al Awad almost swoon with emotion as he explored the ancient document.

Slowly, he removed a white glove and ran one of his fingers along the side of the manuscript page, making contact with Assemani's ink. A deep sense of loss and rage suddenly came over him. All the history that belonged and did not belong to him. All that he could access but not claim, duplicate but not possess.

Unsettled, he put his glove back on. Then walked to the darkroom and started work, meticulously photographing the first ornate page of the manuscript. In total darkness, he filled three trays — developer, stop bath and fixer — then opened the holder and plunged the negative into the first tray, and gently shook the container. He immersed it in more chemicals, before completing a good wash of the negative. He left this to dry in the film closet, left his office for the day, and slowly walked out of the library into the bright evening light and fresh air. He strolled to Sophia's, a nearby restaurant, for some food and a glass of beer. Only the proprietor's stories and the trashy local journal (which he enjoyed despite feeling he should not) offered him an escape from his own existence, which, he thought suddenly, so often felt anachronistic.

Over the front door to Al Awad's apartment building, an eagle was prominently engraved. The residence, once grand but now in a state of genteel disrepair, had been built by its owner, a Parsi from India, who for many years had lived alone in the penthouse. He had died after an accident, a quiet fall in his apartment, and was discovered dead in his kitchen some weeks later. A part of his body had been consumed by crows who'd gained access through the balcony and come inside to eat the man's remains.

Al Awad kept very few books at home; he had never

needed to amass a library of his own since he had always worked in the catacombs of one reading room or another. He was paid relatively well but led a frugal, melancholic existence, weathering constant regret that he had appeared in the world only after all the great thinkers and prophets had long gone. In his youth, his contempt for modern life had led him to his current state: dwelling in the permanence of the obscure. Years ago, he had constructed long wooden panels, painted them black and placed them so that they blocked the windows, as if to replicate a dungeon or a hermit's cave. He had also done this out of a fear of birds, particularly scavengers like those that had devoured the Parsi owner of the building.

The next morning, through a strange series of events, Al Awad entered a new phase of life, a phase of doubt.

Back in the darkroom, he retrieved the four-by-five negative from the night before and stretched his arm out against the light. To his astonishment, the negative that he had copied from the Assemani-annotated manuscript showed the name of Jesus substituted with the name Simon Magus. He read this quickly twice, then carried the negative to the table for a more thorough examination. After studying it with his pocket magnifier, there was no doubt: the name of Simon Magus leaped out at him. This was certainly out of context — and, equally concerning to Al Awad, he couldn't recall having seen this name at all when he had photographed that section of the text the day before.

He rushed back to the archive, asked the librarian for the manuscript, and located the relevant paragraph and line. The name of Jesus appeared clearly on the script; the name Simon Magus did not. Al Awad felt queasy, but with an effort, he composed himself. He would re-enter the darkroom and make a printout of the negative in his hand. Fifteen minutes later, the print, to his amazement, bore the name of Jesus, and there was no sign or trace of Simon Magus. Methodically applying Cartesian logic, Al Awad reviewed all the steps in his procedures. Finding nothing he could fault himself for, he looked for other paragraphs in the manuscript that might contain the name Simon Magus. But nothing could explain the mystery. Then, though it would inevitably produce a lower-quality copy, he hit upon the ingenious idea to duplicate the negative itself. But when he made this copy, the result was even more maddening and devastating: not only was Simon Magus no longer to be found on the second negative, but the name had now been replaced by that of Waraqa Ibn Nawfal, the Nestorian priest who was first cousin of both the prophet Muhammad and Khadija, who became the first wife of the Prophet.

Terror took hold of Al Awad. Was he suffering a psychotic episode or delusional disorder?

He would take a walk and get some fresh air.

A short time later, he was sitting in the same chair at the same table at the same restaurant, Sophia's Place, where he had dined last night. Sophia herself waited on him.

As she bustled around Al Awad's table, Sophia complained about Moustafa, the Indian Muslim whose business empire had grown and grown. Now he was trying to take over her restaurant too. Moustafa, she alleged, had started as a delivery boy at a small store owned by a woman twice his age named Khadima. Then, one day, Khadima's uncle suggested a marriage of convenience to the delivery boy. A couple of years after the wedding, the uncle died, and Khadima died soon after, and Moustafa inherited the store and two other buildings. He sold one of them and expanded his property business with the help of his shady cousins. Moustafa had turned from a sweet, illiterate, fatherless boy into an expansionist entrepreneur. And now he's aiming to acquire my restaurant too, Sophia concluded. I am not envious of his wealth, but the neighbourhood has changed.

Al Awad listened in silence, and after he had finished his meal, he walked slowly home.

On the way, a homeless man stopped him and said, For ten dollars, I can give you my secret knowledge. My name is Simon, and I am a magus, a magician. I am also capable of flight.

The smell of the man's body made Al Awad nauseous, and he involuntarily stepped back. As if he could read Al Awad's mind, the magus declared: The universe is a pigsty, and the light you seek is elsewhere. Then, suddenly, he disappeared, as if he was indeed capable of flight.

The baffling events of the day had made Al Awad tired, and back in his room, he arranged the black panels against all sources of light, and fell into a slumber, not waking until he heard the voice of a neighbour calling her kids to get ready for school. He got up and rushed back to the library, hoping that all of yesterday's events had been a dream. He pulled the negatives again, and a chill swept over his body.

There had been no illusion. The alternative names were still there, in all their variant forms.

In desperation, Al Awad went through his process one more time, copying the last negative he had made. Then he stepped back in horror: it was his own name that now appeared.

That night, all night, he cried and trembled inside the dark confinement of his chamber.

Obsessively, he went back over every encounter he'd had since the first substitute name had appeared. Slowly it dawned on him that everything that had appeared on the negatives was somehow related to his own recent experiences. And now that his own name had also appeared on the negative, there must be a mysterious message he needed to decode, an alle-gorical statement of sorts. Had his present existence and a parallel world of the past finally intersected? Perhaps a past history, latent until now, was making itself manifest in his own present in the same way that a photographic print, a positive, makes itself known by way of the negative.

Sophia's account of the Indian grocer Moustafa recalled to Al Awad's mind the story of the prophet Muhammad, and his transition from a caravan worker to a husband and consequently a great conqueror. And the homeless man on the road recalled the life of the Christian heretic of the same name, Simon Magus, arguably the founder of Gnosticism. But no matter how hard he tried to find an explanation or parallel, the appearance of Al Awad's own name on the negative remained a complete mystery, and a frightening one.

Back at the archive the next day, he tried one more desperate act: he duplicated the last negative, the negative that carried his name. This time, when he held up the result, no name appeared at all — only a blank white space, utterly white and translucent.

The next day, Al Awad was found dead in his bed, his white-gloved hands holding an achromatic duplicate of the Assemani manuscript. The library was obliged to report to the Vatican that the original had been misplaced.

Over the years to follow, many papers were written about the mysterious disappearance of the manuscript. Some experts feared that the original was lost for good. Many surmised, in long articles and theses, that Al Awad had tried to forge a false negative, a black-and-white script that pretended to be a faithful copy but in fact introduced the names of various dead figures alongside his own. As scholars mourned the absence of the original manuscript, this negative of Al Awad's was invariably considered inferior, a small part of a standard process of production, no object of art or particular interest.

And so it was that Al Awad's negative remained deep in the archive department of the university library, where it possessed an aura all its own, free from the processes of reproduction.

THE WAVE

THERE IS A DISASTER COMING, and for the past twenty years I've been warning the authorities about it. No one believes me — but it will happen. It will happen tomorrow, July 9. The first tidal wave will hit the shore at 3:45 p.m. sharp. The location? The Beirut shore.

The tidal wave will decimate my place of birth, and I am excited to watch it happen.

Let me introduce myself. My name is Ghassan El-Hajjar and I am a geologist and ex–university professor. I graduated with a PhD in geoscience from the University of Calgary, Canada. My dissertation was on earthquakes and their aftermaths. I studied the relationships between mountain thrust faults, plate tectonics, sea floor landslides and tidal waves. I have spent most of my life in pursuit of historical occurrences of tidal waves or, to use the Roman word, *brasmatia*, which literally means the shaking of the earth. Nor do I exclude from my vocabulary the more current term: *tsunami*. As I already mentioned, I am an ex-professor and for the last fifteen years I've been waiting, with anticipation, for this big event: the wave.

As a child, I was fascinated by the fact that Beirut, in the year AD 551, during the reign of the Roman emperor Justinian I, was destroyed by a series of gigantic tidal waves. And I lived with the fear of another tsunami. The idea of losing my city and my family to a large quantity of water horrified me.

That fascination and horror triggered my interest in geology, which I pursued from an early age. My father, who was an enlightened man, encouraged me. He provided me with books and read to me with delighted pride. The small globe that he bought me was the only thing that I kept when I left the country of my birth in 1990, at the age of twenty. As a child, I would pretend to fly above the globe while reciting the names of all the countries of the world, their main cities and capitals. It was a game that my father and I often played. As for my mother, when I was very young, the sight of my father and me extending our arms and spinning the globe always brought a smile to her face; but when I reached my teens, the idea of me studying something so irrelevant to the world we lived in alarmed her. And the certainty that I would leave to complete my degree in a foreign land brought tears to her eyes.

My ideas about air and flight were certainly positive. My ideas about water, on the other hand, had been peculiar ever since I'd learned of its devastating effect on people and their homes. Baths were out of the question for me, although I did tolerate showers. The water reservoirs commonly found on rooftops were a necessity I accepted, though I periodically climbed to our rooftop to check for signs of rust or cracks that might result in leaks. During family trips to the beach, I would stand on a chair and watch the horizon for large waves and listen for the sound of rumblings from the deep. My fear was instinctive and may even have preceded my formal study of water. During my baptism, I was told, I refused to let the priest submerge me in the basin. My godfather and godmother had to bend my knees and force my head down in order for the ritual to be completed.

As an adult, I felt called to research and meticulously document the effects of tidal waves through history. This led me to conclude that tsunamis are cyclical — and not just cyclical, but recurring like clockwork, able to be predicted to the second. Now, you may think I am mad. No worries — so did my colleagues at the geosciences department where I taught for many years before I was denied tenure and eventually dismissed. When I applied for the position, the hiring committee had been intrigued by the ideas I presented: ideas about cycles in nature and human development, and how recurrence is related, for humans, to perceptions of the transcendental. In my interview, I impressed the committee with my multidisciplinary presentation on recurrence as metaphor, and I even introduced a new term: "Transcendental Geography: The Role of Natural Events on Human Systems of Belief and Evolution." I suspect my emphasis on my Eastern identity enhanced, in my colleagues' eyes, my theological arguments. Naturally, the fools gobbled it all up. I played my cards skilfully, injecting my presentation with historical, cultural, anthropological and theological references, but in truth, the whole thing was a deception. I had no intention of integrating any of this postmodern multidisciplinary rubbish into my work. My sole purpose in life, back then, was to save lives and cities from drowning and submersion. I took my work very seriously and my approach was always pragmatic, rational and, above all, free of any religious belief.

After I won the position, I gave an important lecture about the formation of temporal patterns and the accumulation of metallic layers beneath the earth's surface and could feel the disappointment. My lecture was, in the view of the academic community, regrettably scientific and systematic. But the big controversy came later, when I proclaimed that I could predict coming disasters to the minute, even to the second. That's when the mockery, hostility and accusations started. Those wretched scholars turned against me. My colleagues in the department were worse than gluttonous Roman senators, raising their heavy fists as I entered meetings and throwing their intellectual daggers at my body, eventually destroying my career. They even dragged my protege in to take a shot at me. In time, these malicious professors ensured my tenure was denied. Eventually, I was forced to leave the department, and my life took a downturn.

I moved to Montreal and took a job as a low-level bureau-crat at city hall. I passed many years doing minor tasks in an office filled with petty officials whose sole enjoyment in life was to accumulate little victories and score small gains with their inconsequential powers. I watched them routinely berating citizens for failing to closely read forms; I watched them jeer at incomplete applications. Oh, how many tidal waves I've wished upon my colleagues. I called forth from the Alaska Panhandle the 1958 Lituya Bay tsunami with its 30.6 million cubic metres of water to fall upon the head of Réjean, that bald, miserable sycophant with his pitiful lunch box and his meek ten o'clock coffee. I summoned the 1755 Lisbon earthquake and tsunami to humiliate that fat-assed pseudo-intellectual Gaétan, who never stopped reminding everyone of his post-secondary education. Once, Gaétan saw me with a book and in his dismissive way asked what I was reading.

Kant, I replied.

He smiled and said sardonically, What about him?

I am reading an essay by Kant, published in the Königsberg newspaper, on the Lisbon earthquake.

Oh, and what about it? Gaétan said, mocking me with his facetious interest.

The German philosopher describes how pretentious, mis-erable idiots deserve to die by natural disasters above all other causes because that is the most just way to remind them how insignificant they are, I replied. Of course, I made this up, but I think Gaétan understood my meaning.

One thing redeemed my job: it led me to Marie, my future wife. She was working as a self-employed translator from French to English. We communicated a few times by email, and I sent her text that needed translation, mostly brochures about cultural activities and local community events, as well as educational literature. And then, one day, having never seen her in person, I asked if she would like to join me for a coffee. I knew she would not refuse a meeting with her main client, the city. At the café, I immediately apologized for using my position at city hall for personal ends. And then I asked her out. She told me she liked my accent and that my nose reminded her of an equilateral triangle, and she laughed. Later, I told her about the geological research I was now conducting independent of any institution. That appealed to her as much as my accent and my nose. She confided to me that deep down she was a bit of an anarchist herself, and that her only shame was that she needed money, which is why she had to work for the city, an institution she deeply mistrusted.

We started seeing each other on a regular basis. I cooked for Marie, and she discovered she loved the taste of Lebanese food. After a few months of dating, I told her that I had decided to quit my job and go home for a year to research tidal waves and the phenomenon of their recurrence. I explained to her that only in Lebanon could I conduct the necessary research on the tsunami of July 9, AD 551, during Roman rule of the region.

Marie didn't know much about the history of my homeland — or even that the Romans had occupied this part of the world centuries ago. Like a Buddhist, she took pride in living in the present, as she often tried to tell me. Her circle was mostly artists — but the kind I considered pseudo-artists, devoid of intellectual discourse. Some made costume jewellery, or *faux bijoux* as it is known in Montreal; others did pottery; some were environmentalists; all were health conscious and believed in niceness as a way of living. Her crowd was very different from the uptight academics and dispirited bureaucrats I had previously spent most of my time with. Smoking drugs and playing the guitar soon became our weekend ritual. And gradually, Nature became an unexpected part of my life, along with walks, composting, recycling, tofu and other unsatisfying natural ingredients, not to speak of handmade soaps.

Marie's favourite friends were a man named Rodrigues and his wife, Helena, both from Chile, and both in their fifties when we met. Marie never stopped reminding me that they had been forced to come to Montreal because of General Pinochet. Another friend was a woman called Mathilde, a flake who was into astrology and planetary alignments, and who was the most annoying of Marie's circle. Once, at a party, I had a heated argument with Astro-Mathilde. Marie was

upset that I had insulted her friend, and for a week, she didn't
return my calls. Then I bumped into her on the street, and she
came back to my place. We fucked, and afterwards she told
me that she had almost no one in this world but her friends.
They were her real family, and if I couldn't tolerate them, I
should leave her alone. Besides, she said, just because you've
showed me and my friends all your scientific data doesn't
mean that you are right about your own predictions and ideas
about nature.

Six months later, just as I was about to leave for Beirut, Marie
and I spontaneously and, I should add, *mysteriously* got
married. We'd had a few drinks and then got high, and there
was a great, unexplainable intimacy between us that night.
I proposed out of the blue, and Marie laughed and said:
"Only if we go to Beirut for a honeymoon."

"It is dangerous there," I said.

"And what's an adventure without the possibility of
danger?"

I agreed. I promised that we would go. And Marie smiled.

And so, in the year 2015, I was subjected to an excruciating
marriage ceremony. The wedding itself seemed like an exotic
ritual that made me want to laugh. We were married in Marie's
sister's garden in a small village in northern Quebec. The
Chilean couple jointly performed the ceremony in Spanish.

I didn't understand a word, but simply accepted Spanish as the new universal language. Rodrigues and Helena wore loose cotton clothing in bright colours and many ornaments in their hair and ears and around their necks. In my suit, I looked like a CEO at a hippie gathering. Marie's friends had decorated the garden and lit incense through the house and in the back porch where the ceremony took place. The food was vegetarian. I paid for everything, including the airfare for the honeymoon and a fee for the rental of the sister's backyard. But as strange as all this was to me, I was happy. For once, I was carefree and not thinking about the future. And the prospect of going back to Beirut with a Western wife was amusing. I had resigned a few days before from my job at the city and felt a buoyant lightness.

After the reception, we drove to a nearby lake, where Marie and her friends lit a large bonfire. We held hands and recited an incantation, celebrating life and death. Then everyone else stripped nude and jumped in the water, and I stood at the shore in my suit, but without shoes, the hemline of my pants where they reached the top of my ankles soaked in the last reach of the waves.

The purpose of the visit to Lebanon was for me to conduct further research on mountain thrust faults, plate tectonics and tidal wave formation, and for Marie to experience the

East for the first time. Sometimes now I wonder if that was the only reason she accepted my marriage proposal.

When we arrived in Lebanon, we stayed in the capital for a few weeks and then we headed up to the mountainous regions. We rented a house in a little village called Aytabeit. The name must have originated in the Syriac language; the word, in that dead language, meant a village and a house, I explained to Marie. But history doesn't mean anything to me, she replied, my interest is in the people of the village. In her colourful, hippie-like cotton robes and sandals, she would stroll through the village greeting everyone. And the villagers would ask her all kinds of questions and offer her fruit, drinks and hospitality. I tried to warn her about revealing things to the villagers, tried to tell her they were nothing but gossip receptacles. But she insisted on absorbing the culture. She accused me of always being suspicious and said that I had no trust in people's goodness. She much preferred the authentic villagers to pretentious city people. When she had met members of my family in Beirut, she'd thought they were too Western, too cosmopolitan, too bourgeois — and the more they tried to impress her with drinks, food and the famously decadent Beirut scene, the more she resented my family and eventually me. In the village, she was invited for coffee and sweets, and that pleased her tremendously.

But one day, the grocer refused to call me Professor because, he said, I had been kicked out of the university. I knew then that the villagers had pulled everything about me from my naive wife. I was furious. How dare these vicious peasants intrude into my life? When Marie came home, I told her how furious I was.

That night, in our little house in the village, my wife called me a bourgeois; she accused me of being a Third World elite — a Frenchman! she said. She told me she was upset with me because I treated the poor villagers with arrogance.

I called her naive. I told her that, during the civil war, these villagers had committed massacres. There was nothing innocent about them. I considered telling her about my childhood. Instead, I said, All these farmers and villagers are cunning. They are skilled at extracting information from others and never revealing any of their own, and they menace each other with their customs, politeness and archaic norms. There is nothing but treachery in them, I said. She had been duped by her need to exoticize these people. There was nothing noble about any of them. They had pulled guns on each other and slaughtered their neighbours. Everyone is capable of harm, I shouted. I called her out on her silly spirituality and her flaky New Age so-called family. This is real life here, I declared. The war in Syria is only a few villages away. The fundamentalists might approach sooner than we think and any of us could be slaughtered.

Marie called me a monster, a reactionary who blames the oppressed. And then she, like the rest of the world, mocked me and my prophecies of the coming tidal wave. "And if your disaster predictions are not fundamentalist, what is?" she screamed at me. "I, unlike you, embrace death and the inevitable necessity of change. I see it and I walk towards it. But you are a coward, living out a fantasy of saving the world. So let the warriors and the waves come, what are you afraid of?"

That's when she opened the door and left. I thought she would go for a short walk and come back, as she always did when we fought. I didn't wait for her return but fell fast asleep on the couch.

In the morning, I heard bells and then the screams of women. I saw the men take their guns and cars and speed down the narrow roads, merging with more guns and cars in the centre of the village until it was impossible to move. They are coming! everyone shouted. The Islamists are on their way. They have already crossed the border.

Leave everything and run, a soldier yelled into a loud-speaker. Do not pack, do not look back. Another soldier, unarmed, stood on top of a jeep and declared: Those men who are willing to stay behind and carry arms should come with me. Those who remain behind are staying to fight. They are giving their family and kids the chance to escape, but they will not escape themselves. As he said these words, women held on to their husbands, fathers and sons and begged them to leave the village. But many men would not, and some pushed away their wives and daughters, forcing them alone into cars or the back of other villagers' trucks.

I looked for Marie, but she was nowhere to be seen.

I walked through the village, shouting Marie's name. An old woman whom my wife had visited came towards me. She had seen Marie going up the hill. I warned her not to go that way, the old woman said, but she didn't listen, and she kept on walking towards the invaders.

Behind me, the villagers were now heading towards the valley and even farther down the mountain to the shore. Later, I was told that the priest who stayed behind saw Marie and ran after her. He spoke to her in French and told her to go back to her husband and to leave the village. Marie ignored him and took the opposite road.

I lost her. I simply lost her. I stayed behind for as long as I could, looking for her, hoping she would turn back and I would find her, but eventually, late that afternoon, the fighters came to me and said, Professor, either you carry a gun or you must leave. By now, your wife is either captured or dead.

Another fighter added, If she is lucky, they will spare her and name her Meriam. And he and his friends chuckled.

I have already determined exactly where the wave will hit and at what time. It will hit Beirut tomorrow afternoon, July 9, at 3:45 p.m., and as I have already mentioned to you, I am very happy about the prospect of seeing the city I once considered my own destroyed by wave after wave from the belly of the Mediterranean Sea — or what the Romans called Mare Nostrum — with its discharge of salt water and debris. This city is nothing now but a hub for a deranged sect of fundamentalists who twelve years ago managed to sweep through the mountains and down the coast, repeating the inevitable: the sacking of Rome by Germanic tribes, the destruction of Baghdad by the Mongols, the defeat of the Americans in Vietnam by the Communists of the North.

I have witnessed it all. I witnessed the city's fall and the exodus of every religious minority. I watched boats and planes rushing out of the country for months on end until the loss was complete. And those who didn't make it — well, their fate was sealed.

I managed to leave, but tomorrow I will return, flying over this city as I once imagined flying over the globe my father gave me. Most of the earth is covered by oceans, by the sea, he would tell me, and as a child, I would worry that the rest of the orb would soon be covered by blue too.

Tomorrow, as the first wave approaches the shore, I will be above Beirut, seeing it for the last time, recording the approach of the water to the exact millisecond. The first wave will devastate the shore, the second will obliterate the city from existence. I have asked the pilot to time it so that we will be right above the water, with a bird's-eye view. The wave will hit the shore in the afternoon, just as bearded warriors and their wives stroll along the boardwalk we used to call the Corniche. I will watch the inhabitants of my ancient city gasp for air from under the weight of liquid and prayers.

And yes, my wife Marie might be there, holding a child in one arm and guiding another with her hand. And yes, inevitably, when the wave comes, she will be walking towards it.

THE COLOUR OF TREES

UNTIL HIS RETIREMENT, Professor James Aesthia taught at Concordia University in Montreal, where for four decades he had lectured in the Faculty of Philosophy on a particularly obscure branch of Ethics and Aesthetics — using a course title he secretly loved for the confusion caused by its closeness to his own surname. He had a predilection for subtle eccentric humour.

On the last day of his career, before making his way to the retirement party his colleagues had organized, he packed up his few remaining books and belongings: a mug for tea given to him by his late wife, an old poster for a conference he'd once organized in Paris, his collection of pencils, erasers and his old mechanical pencil sharpener. Then, in a melancholic moment, he realized that of all the books and papers he had accumulated over the years, the only thing that would remain after his retreat from professional view was their dust — invisible to his eyes for so long, but now so prevalent.

After living for decades with dust in a distant office at the end of a long hall, where the small single window afforded a view of the sky only when he stood on a chair and craned his neck to look out over the university gates and road below, he decided to relocate to his late wife's village, where the air was fresh and nature could provide him with all the good things he had missed experiencing in the city during his working life. He reluctantly recalled Heidegger, whose political choices, made during the Third Reich, had complicated the professor's relationship with the work of Heidegger the philosopher who'd lived in nature. The professor's wife had bequeathed him her family cottage, however, and so he shipped his office library to the property, sold his apartment in Montreal, and decided to dedicate himself to a simple life of contemplation, reading and solitary walks.

For his first two weeks in the cottage, the professor kept expecting his wife to reappear. Everything reminded him of her joyful, noisy upkeep of the house and garden. She had been a farmer's daughter, well versed in the persistent and unforgiving demands of nature, whereas he had heralded from an old aristocratic lineage (if, he thought wryly, one was permitted to acknowledge such a thing in North America). Soon he remembered his wife's favourite spot, the clifftops overlooking the valley below, with sublime views of the surrounding mountains. He made his way there to look out at the big Canadian sky and the magnitude of the land before him.

That first fall, he took the turning of the leaves amid the Indian summer as assurance that he had made the right choice to retire to this secluded part of the world, if only to witness the beauty of the death of the foliage, the spectacular colours, the bright mourning of the trees for better days, the endless transforming processions of the cycle of life. During this short period, he felt much happiness, and his now habitual walks towards the cliffs were filled with exuberance and a sense of purpose. Few people came to the spot when he did — only the odd few teenagers, smoking and kissing, or a clandestine couple who would watch the valley from the seats of their car, or the occasional lone male standing beside a vehicle, there to look at the view.

Professor James Aesthia, in his full retirement attire of winter coat, hat and cane — an addition to his carefully cultivated persona of a man of a certain era and style — could regularly be seen standing at the cliff edge, observing the picturesque view as the sinking sun radiated the colours of its descent, enhancing the orange of the leaves at the hour of the *crépuscule*. He acquired a pipe and some tobacco from the village nearby, and found that the new persona he had constructed for himself pleased him. His subtle eccentric humour often surfaced in a playful awareness of his own image, his character of the self. And in fact, he considered himself a solipsist, an epistemological position that he had kept secret, hidden from his university colleagues for those years in the city, and one that he held in spite of all the knowledge he had accrued and all the books he had read. The universe before his eyes, beautiful and wondrous as it was, did nothing to convince him that there was anything to discover beyond the self, the inner world that limited our relations with the outside world. How destructive and alienating, he thought, was that dialectical relation between the inner world of the self and the outer self of the world.

Perhaps this was what lay at the heart of his decision to retreat to such a remote place. The best the outside world could offer the professor was the spectacle of a few changes and fleeting colours.

One day towards the end of autumn, the professor was standing at his regular lookout when he saw a couple of teenagers, a boy and a girl, rushing towards the cliff's edge to take a selfie against the vast backdrop. The boy leaned dramatically, his phone in his outstretched arm, as they both giggled and smiled, repositioning the angles of their bodies, standing alarmingly close to the edge. The girl's foot stepped over into oblivion and then she slipped backwards and clutched at her boyfriend instinctively, her arm already tightly wound around his neck, and they both lost balance and fell — it all happened in an instant — off the cliff and into the abyss. Gone.

The professor stood there in shock. Only after a moment did he understand what had happened. He ran towards the edge of the cliff and looked down, but couldn't see anything of the couple, only small particles of dust rising, somehow confirming the scale of the tragedy. He panted in horror, lay flat on his stomach and began screaming into the valley. He screamed and shouted until another couple, one he had noticed previously and imagined to be on an illicit tryst, ran from their vehicle and joined him in his screams. The man even tried to clamber down the cliff, but its face was sheer, too steep, too dangerous; he rushed to his car and called the police and then the three witnesses paced along the edge of the cliff like panting tigers in a cage, absorbing the tragic fate of two young people, the terror of it — although only the professor had seen them fall. Horrible, horrible, the professor shouted, and the woman began to cry, and the man continued to patrol the edge and off to the side, trying to find a view down, shuffling, hesitant, panicked. Finally, the three of them collapsed on the ground to wait for help to come.

In the fading light, the police arrived. They asked the professor a few questions as mountaineers secured ropes and descended into the abyss.

The professor, devastated as he sat in the back of the police car, said the same phrase over and over, "Senseless death, oh, this senseless existence." More cars arrived, and soon journalists and photographers appeared. The identity of the young couple, the victims, was announced not long after.

For the next few months, the professor locked himself in his home, barely setting foot outside, no longer walking up to the clifftop view his late wife had so loved. "The self," he recited, as he paced around his little cottage, numb. "The self," he would repeat as he walked about in his private state of madness, "the self. The treachery of it all." He stopped reading altogether and sometimes sat at the window looking at his own reflection in the glass until the outside light dimmed and faded entirely, and then he would go to bed.

After a few months, once the snow had come and covered all that had passed, the professor felt able to walk towards the cliff again, and so he reinstated his earlier routine. But now, instead of admiring the view, he would stand and shiver and challenge the harsh winter wind. "I defy you, I defy you. I won't idly cherish your treacherous sunset colours, and all your fall beauty," he would rage, talking directly to the cliff face and sometimes shouting into the valley beneath. Later, he would walk back, soaking wet, and stand in his kitchen sopping, and start a fire.

Spring and summer came and went, and fall came round again. The professor noticed that the cliff had become a tourist attraction popular with Japanese people who travelled all the way from their distant islands to witness the slow-motion death of the leaves, the killer conquest of their colours, the grand illusion of tranquility and peace it conveyed. He began to time his daily visit to coincide with that of the tourists, and would watch them coming down from their bus coaches and rushing towards the cliff of death, its perilous rim still exposed. Whenever he saw men or women extending their arms to smile at their devices, he would race to intercede and ask if they would like him to take a photo for them. Many did, gladly handing him their phones, as his age and his dandy's clothes projected decency and inspired trust, and he would walk towards them with his cane, asking them to move towards him and away, away from the edge.

In time, he started to talk at more leisure to the many people who loved to take in the progress of the changing colours. He talked and talked. Slowly his long monologues would unfurl. His life stories took hold of him, and whenever he held a tourist phone in his hand, he would recount a variation of the following words: "I remember the day in Tuscany with my wife when I walked to Siena cathedral, I remember seeing Michelangelo's self-portrait. He was standing front and centre in the frame, looking young and proud of himself. He looked playful too, with his red hair and boyish looks. It was then I understood the great joke about the self. It was then I understood the root of that moment of celebration of one's own self. It's not due to the attention one commands, or one's humour, but, I realized, it is the exclusion of everything except oneself. Michelangelo in that portrait is all that there is — just like a saint's halo is a rejection of everything else surrounding it; it is all that there is. I might also add, ladies and gentlemen, that it's a confirmation of all that we don't control, all that is not relevant, an affirmation of the deep sense of estrangement that we manifest in our laughter and playfulness. The exclusive forms of our representations of the self reveal the sadness in our relationship with this universe. For all the landscapes that Van Gogh painted, his most brutal and articulate expressions were his self-portraits executed at a forensically close proximity, in total disregard of all that is before us, above us and below us . . . The tragic self is all there is, and all that is around us is mere colour and illusion. These cameras of yours, these manifestations of our fraught relation to technology and the mechanization of the world, these deadly little devices, should be abandoned. I shall save you from them, and from confrontation with their interplanetary and satellite technology. Yes, this should all stop . . . The gaze within should contain no image of the outer world, but bear only a true reflection of the self, of what is always there, not a superficial overview of the self, but the self in all its depths. I must also say that nature reveals itself in — But now I have to tell you another story of my Tuscan voyage . . . My wife . . . and her friend . . . had a camera and I thought . . ."

As time went on, the professor's monologues grew longer and increasingly convoluted, and sometimes he screamed his speeches. One day, he refused to give his captive audience of tourists their phones back, and they became hostage to a particularly long, incomprehensible soliloquy. When a tour guide tried to take back the phones by force, the professor swung his cane in the air and threatened the group, roaring Heidegger at them all: "Everywhere we remain unfree and chained to technology, whether we passionately affirm or deny it."

The police were called and escorted him to their vehicle.

Following this incident and his arrest, Professor James Aesthia was periodically taken for psychological assessment. One fall day a couple of years later, he was committed to a nearby institution with a view of the valley and surrounded by trees. There, in his room, he could be seen scribbling papers and writing pretentiously in a large notebook. He no longer responded to his own name but spoke only in German. For a time, he insisted on being called Martin, and then demanded to be addressed by all parties as Professor Heidegger. Many of the staff sardonically called him Emeritus Professor Heidy.

Upon examination of his notebook after his death, it was revealed that Professor James Aesthia had been in the process of completing the autobiography of Heidegger in the form of a journal. It was composed of a long monologue supposedly recited by Heidegger on one of his nature outings, while standing at the edge of Eagle's Nest near the Berghof and Obersalzberg in the Bavarian Alps. The monologue involved a long justification of why he had chosen to become a fascist collaborator. In this text, Heidegger presented himself as an old man with a cane and gave scrupulous details of his clothing and his daily walks to the clifftop for fresh air. The abundant nature he observed filled the first half of the journal alongside endless descriptions of pristine views. In the second half of the narrative, Heidegger was captured by the Allies and confined to a room, forced to write his confessions. The room held a desk, a bed, a mirror and a television. A guard brought him food and then escorted the philosopher, in chains, to the bathroom at the end of the hallway. Heidegger's confession was to be conducted facing a mirror containing a technological device that would trigger the recording only when he stood directly before the glass and stated his full name.

Heidegger — through an elaborate, but never apologetic, written confession — then reveals that he collaborated with the Nazis not because of professional ambition but rather because he saw an opportunity to carry out his studies on technology and the emptiness of being without weapons and tools; and also to explore the fullness of being when we become an extension of our technological nature. In the professor's notebook, Heidegger regrets his glorification of technology and demands that the facility's staff take the TV and all other devices out of his room. Nothing is done, however, and one evening, in a fit of rage, the philosopher Heidy manages to prise open his cell's window using a knife and fork. He lifts the TV onto a rolling tray, transports it across the room and throws it out of the window, watching as it falls to the ground below. As punishment for his actions, the journal recounts, Heidegger is imprisoned in a room filled with televisions running continuously, showing images of high mountains with birds circling their peaks, and of people boarding trains.

The professor's will stated that his archive and library were to be donated to the philosophy faculty at his old university. As for the rest of his assets, these were to be liquidated and bequeathed to the local authority, with certain conditions.

One year after the professor's death, the town erected a safety ledge around the cliff. And soon after, as autumn leaves began to turn, a beautiful garden and simple memorial attracted visitors. Its commemorative plaque — with a portrait of a young couple — read: *For those who flew ahead, only to wait for us at the edge of a beautiful eternity.*

ACKNOWLEDGEMENTS

With gratitude to Charles Buchan, Sarah Chalfant, Lynn Henry
and Madeleine Thien.